GHOSTROOTS

GHOSTROOTS

stories

'Pemi Aguda

W. W. NORTON & COMPANY
Independent Publishers Since 1923

These stories were previously published, in slightly different form, in the following publications: "Manifest" (*Granta*), "Breastmilk" (*One Story*; reprinted in *The Best Short Stories 2022: The O. Henry Prize Winners*, edited by Valeria Luiselli), "Contributions" (*American Short Fiction*), "The Hollow" and "24, Alhaji Williams Street" (*Zoetrope: All Story*; "The Hollow" was reprinted in *The Best Short Stories 2023: The O. Henry Prize Winners*, edited by Lauren Groff), "Imagine Me Carrying You" (*Ploughshares*), "Things Boys Do" (*Nightmare Magazine*), "Birdwoman" (*Omenana Magazine*), "The Dusk Market" (*Zyzzyva*), and "Masquerade Season" (*Tor.com*)

For information about permission to reproduce selections from this book, write to Permissions, W. W. Norton & Company, Inc., 500 Fifth Avenue, New York, NY 10110

For information about special discounts for bulk purchases, please contact W. W. Norton Special Sales at specialsales@wwnorton.com or 800-233-4830

Manufacturing by Lakeside Book Company
Book design by Beth Steidle
Production manager: Lauren Abbate

ISBN 978-1-324-06585-2

W. W. Norton & Company, Inc., 500 Fifth Avenue, New York, N.Y. 10110
www.wwnorton.com

W. W. Norton & Company Ltd., 15 Carlisle Street, London W1D 3BS

1 2 3 4 5 6 7 8 9 0

For Modupe and Ngozi, and the women who raised me

CONTENTS

Manifest 1

Breastmilk 23

Contributions 45

The Hollow 51

Imagine Me Carrying You 67

24, Alhaji Williams Street 87

Things Boys Do 105

Birdwoman 117

Girlie 125

The Wonders of the World 149

The Dusk Market 175

Masquerade Season 189

Acknowledgments 205

GHOSTROOTS

MANIFEST

THIS IS THE FIRST PIMPLE OF YOUR LIFE. QUESTION THE foreign object with all your fingers.

If you were to draw a straight line down from the right corner of your lip, then another straight line forward from the corner of your jaw, the pimple would be sitting at that intersection. Your index fingernail—false, acrylic, painted a burnt orange—flicks at the tiny bump. You press the pad of your thumb down on it, hard. The pimple does not go away. You have just turned twenty-six, why now?

Tonight, your mother calls you Agnes for the first time.

Agnes is not your name.

You are sitting at the dining table, picking beans, picking at this pimple. You like to sort beans on the wide surface of the mahogany table that's older than you, sliding weevils and broken beans to a corner, making a route through the good beans so that you never have to lift them up. You think of the bad beans and weevils as lepers, driven out of the colony to live amongst themselves in disease and brokenness forever. When a weevil starts to creep back to the good beans, you stab at it. You love to feel them die. The crunch, then the give, under the force of your finger. Flick the dead off, stab again. Your mother must have been standing there awhile because when you look up, there she is, frozen, gripping her Bible and hymn book bag to the gold buttons of her nineties suit. The illumination from the hallway bulb envelops her so that her edges are blurred. Half of her face eaten by light.

"Agnes?"

"Hmmn?" you ask. "Who's that?" But your mother only shakes her head, retreating.

"Who is Agnes?" you ask your father later that night. He is eating while watching a news report on the South Sudan civil war. *Since the start of the conflict, almost two million people have been internally displaced . . .*

You sit at the foot of his armchair, pulling hairs from your arm in the glow of the television screen. Agnes is your mother's mother, your father tells you. "She died when your mum was young, ṣ'oo mọ ni?" He questions your ignorance as he makes vile noises with his tongue and teeth in an attempt to dislodge beef. But what do Nigerian parents tell their children about their own parents? Especially the Pentecostal Christians? Nothing. If you took a poll of your friends, three out of five would be similarly ignorant of these histories of parents who moved from somewhere to Lagos, left behind religions and curses and distant cousins and grimy pasts.

You ask your father if he wants more beans and beef, your hand back on that pimple. He shakes his head no. Your father hates that you take the weevils out of the beans; he thinks they add a certain flavor to the dish.

◊ ◊ ◊

THE SECOND TIME your mother calls you Agnes, your little family of three is sitting in relative darkness. Electricity is out again and fuel scarcity means that you only see each other in candlelight until the power is restored. Your father snores in the gray-turned-brown armchair you call "Daddy's chair," while you and your mother sit across from each other at the dining table. You pull the empty Milo tin that the candle is mounted on closer to yourself. Wax sloshes off slowly and trickles down a side. You close your left eye, then the right, then the left again, enjoying the way the flame shifts. You draw the candle even closer, sniffing at the flame.

Your mother's face lifts from her phone screen and watches you. Through your left eye, you see her eyes widen. Through your right eye, you see her mouth open. Through both eyes, you see terror spread over her face, the way it does when a flying cockroach is in the vicinity.

"Agnes?" Your mother's voice is all croak and phlegm. "Agnes, is that you?"

You lift the candle to your chin to illuminate, pulling it slightly back when heat licks at that stubborn, still-there, solitary pimple. "It's me." Pause. "Are you okay?"

Your mother says nothing, swallows.

"Mummy, do I look like your mum? Do you look like her?"

She pushes her chair back, not answering, leaving the table in an arthropodous scurry, locking herself in the guest bathroom until the lights come back on.

"But what's wrong with her?" you ask your father the next morning, whispering over his black coffee and your milky tea.

He shrugs. "Her mother died around your age . . . Maybe the resemblance has heightened?" He ruffles his mustache, forehead crinkled. "Be patient with your mum, the memories are hard on her."

◊ ◊ ◊

DAYS LATER, you sit on the four layers of tissue paper you've spread on the toilet seat of one of Lekki's posh restaurants as protection from the innermost liquids of strangers, and stroke at the hardness of the pimple.

You skim the inside headlines of the newspaper you picked from the top of the magazine rack. *Woman Cuts Lover's Penis Off in Rage of Jealousy. Man Beats Daughter to Death for Skipping School. Community in Outskirts of Lagos Hack Thief to Pieces.* You close the paper.

Someone knocks, jiggles the handle, but when you don't respond, footsteps fade away. It is then you wipe with too much tissue, stand. After you flush, your gaze stays fixed inside the toilet bowl even when the shuddering of the machinery has stopped, after the Lekki water is as clear as it will be. You watch until the water in the bowl stills.

The replacement tissue rolls are sitting on an open shelf under the sink. Pick them up, one after the other, throw them into the toilet bowl. All five of them. When the last one has landed on top of the others, white on white on white, squeeze up the newspaper and throw it in too. Flush again. Watch the water rise to seat level. When it starts to seep out of the bowl, through the newspaper's print, and out to the black-and-white hexagonal tiles of the restaurant bathroom, flush one more time. Then walk out of the flooding bathroom.

◊ ◊ ◊

THE NEXT MORNING, you wake up to find the pimple gone. Lying on your back on your friend's sofa, you spread fingers across your face, searching to see if it has moved to a new location. Your unmoisturized fingers are dry and harsh against your soft skin, so you trail every inch lightly, careful not to scratch yourself.

"If you haven't ever had a pimple, can we say you've not gone through puberty?" your friends used to tease you, cupping your cheeks in their hands, plastering kisses on the smooth, taut skin of your face because you have always been the loved baby of the group, the youngest. Sweet baby-faced you.

Only when you are satisfied the bump is no longer there do you creep into the bathroom to stare at your reflection in the tiny mirror above the sink. If you lean back, away from the mirror, you can see all of your face, but no, don't lean back. Move your face up, down, left, right, and see the parts in detail. The thin brows, trimmed too slim by the zealous makeup artist at a friend's wedding. A wide nose, yellow sebaceous dots accenting the point where nose blends into the rest of the face. Lips that are full, too full, so that you highlight with a brown lip liner before filling in with lipstick, an attempt to thin them.

◊ ◊ ◊

THE THIRD TIME your mother called you Agnes, she hit you in the face with a Bible. Your friend Lesley is hosting you until your mother stops seeing her mother in your face, stops labeling you the reincarnation of someone who terrified her. You and Lesley both work on Awolowo Road, so you drive together every morning in the red Honda handed down from your mother. Lesley doesn't have a car.

You move away from the mirror to get ready for work. But

after you have pulled on the branded neon green T-shirt for your job at Globacom, where you spend all your hours asking how you can help customers, the pimple is back. You touch it, softly. It is tiny, almost imperceptible to the eye, but there is a hard bump underneath. You sit on the arm of the sofa that is temporarily your bed, worrying the pimple. Pinch it, press against it.

"Genes," is what you told your friends when they teased. "I got Mama's good skin."

Lesley hasn't stirred from her room this morning. She is a deep sleeper. You stare at your friend's bedroom door, brushing at the pimple. Then you pick up your tote bag. Don't knock on Lesley's door, don't wake her up even though you're her ride to work. Jog down the stairs to your car, slam the door. Drive alone to Awolowo Road with your bag sitting in the passenger seat like a queen.

When Lesley starts to call over and over again, an hour later, sending angry *WTF?!!* texts, turn your phone facedown on the desk. Walk to the bathroom down the hall, lean into the mirror, and see that the pimple is gone again. Your skin is back to baby-smooth and blemish-free.

◊ ◊ ◊

YOU ASK YOUR COWORKERS if they believe in reincarnation. Five of them believe. Two of them claim to have corroborative stories.

One: A man dies from injuries sustained in the Biafra war. His widowed wife gives birth to their son months later. The little boy has dark eyes and an ear split in two, the two parts curling over each other like abandoned twins. The woman traces her son's ear, seeing her husband's blood dripping over her fingers as she cleaned his war wounds.

Two: A man named Collins really wants an education, but he is too old and thick from years on the farm. Collins's farming is successful, though, so when he is bitten by a snake and dies slowly in the arms of his little brother, Eze, he bequeaths his wealth to him, saying he will be back in another life to get an education. Years pass, and when Eze finally has a son after many daughters, people remark that the son loves to lick the palm oil before eating the yam, just like Collins used to. When the son falls ill at the age of ten, Eze consults the dibia, who throws cowries to consult the gods. The gods tell the dibia to tell Eze not to forget that Collins said he would be back for an education. After the boy is enrolled at a school, the strange illness disappears.

"Wow," you say. "Wow." But at lunch, one of the storytellers confesses to you, leaning over your plate of rice and stew, pulling at your sleeve, that he read it all on Nairaland and therefore cannot verify its authenticity.

"Nobody has a story about a reincarnated woman?" you want to know.

"Well, I know I'm Beyoncé," your boss's secretary says, sidling up to you in a haze of flowery perfume.

You frown. "I don't think that's how it works," you tell the woman, who is stroking her blond wig as if it were a living thing, a pet that needs comfort.

"Kilode? I'm telling you I'm Beyoncé. I am Beyoncé." She leans closer to you, her hair falling heavy to brush against your cheek; she caresses your chin, turns it so that she is looking through full false lashes into your brown eyes. She smiles a benevolent smile. "I am Beyoncé."

◊ ◊ ◊

THAT DAY YOU LEFT HOME for Lesley's, your mother returned from choir practice singing a hymn about Jesus and lambs and blood. You were in the kitchen cooking dinner, because you liked to cook, and you liked to cook for your parents, and you liked living with your parents, although you could afford to move, and you liked the cold of the tiles seeping into your feet and the cold of the frozen turkey hurting your fingers.

Your mother's singing stopped when she heard you humming over the sink. She stood at the door to the kitchen, looking at you, her daughter, wearing that black-and-gold kaftan you share. Her Bible trembled in her arms when she spoke.

"Where did you hear that song?"

You turned to squint at her. "What song?"

"What you were humming just now. Where?"

But you couldn't remember what abstract tune it was—from TV? radio?—and you said as much but your mother was already bearing down on you, her terror stark.

"Agnes, why have you come back?"

You stared into your mother's angry eyes, brown and cat-shaped, like yours, with the scanty but long lashes, like yours.

"I'm not Agnes, Mummy. I'm your daughter?" Your voice was small, frightened for the first time since the Agnes episodes began. Her face contorted; her tone, a screech. You leaned away.

"Agnes, why are you back? Have you not done enough evil?"

Then your mother lifted her Bible and swung it through the air until it hit your face. The leather of the Bible stung your chin. "Agnes, I bind you! Agnes, flee, in Jesus's name! Flee!" Your father's voice was somewhere in the background, asking your mother if she'd gone mad. She hit you again and again, turning an eye blood-red, until your father placed his body between you and the Bible. But you did not feel pain, did you? You didn't even flinch. What you felt was a release within you, a stirring, like a cough freeing you from a congestion in your chest.

◊ ◊ ◊

YOU ARE A GOOD GUEST to your friend Amaka, who is hosting you after Lesley told you not to come back to her house. Amaka watched you clean the kitchen, play with her puppy, buy groceries, but her skepticism at your niceness forces a politeness on your interactions that was never there before. Lesley told Amaka about you leaving her that day without any reason or apology, and the gist among your friend group is that you have been acting weird lately, and maybe you are going through something? But Amaka is that friend who doesn't quite know how to say no. "Will you lock up, please?" she asks. "Do you want to use the bathroom first?" Courtesy, as if you've been demoted to acquaintance.

One week into your stay at Amaka's, you wake up to two pimples. One on the same spot on your chin, the other on the left of your eyebrow, like a teenager's bad piercing. The new pimple throbs red, suffusing your head with an ache so intense you think you understand what the coconuts must feel like when you throw them to the ground to break them open in your parents' backyard. You know your head will explode, crack open under this pressure, staining red and white and pink and brown this space you have tried to keep clean for Amaka.

Amaka is not back from work yet, and you sit on the shaggy

rug of her living room, cradling your head in your hands, in your lap. The puppy is nudging your foot, licking your ear. You lift your head, so heavy, and stare into the gray eyes of the small dog that is the size of a handbag, so tiny, so huggable, so cuddle-able, and the dog stares back into your eyes. It has a patch of black around its right eye.

The dog shuffles back. It smells something.

Pick the dog up. The dog is named Ojukwu. Pick it up. Hug the animal tight. Hug the animal tighter until its breath is your breath, and you feel its small bones against your big bones and the breath and the fur are warm against your flushed skin. Hug it even tighter when it starts to scratch at your skin because hugs shouldn't be this tight. Crush the animal until you hear a *pop*, but no, it is not your head that has exploded; your headache, in fact, is now gone—it twitched to a stop along with Ojukwu's heartbeat.

◊ ◊ ◊

YOU CALL YOUR MOTHER'S AUNTIE—one of the four relatives from both parents you're allowed access to—and ask about Agnes. She says: "Oh, I'm surprised your mother told you about her! It can be so hard to talk about. And both of you look like her too, you and your mum—those cheeks, your noses . . . it must be hard to accept. See, Agnes was such a wicked person! Evil! She died really young too, from something too kind like malaria, but everyone was so happy when she was gone."

"But who was she? Where is her family? Mummy never talks about her."

"My dear, nobody knows where my brother married her from. She could be the devil's daughter for all we know! He showed up from a hunting trip with her by his side, not answering any of our questions, unleashing her terror on our family until she killed him finally."

"I didn't know anything about this." The details of your family history are only now beginning to fill in with color, but the colors are harsh, severe, and you're tempted to look away.

"Of what use is it to you, my dear, to know?" your aunt asks. "Let the past stay there, abeg. There are stories we leave buried so our children can move without weight."

"But why?"

"Why what?"

"Agnes. Why was she wicked? What happened to her, to make her be that way?"

Your aunt laughs the way she does when she thinks you've been brainwashed by "the West," like the time you said having house girls was modern slavery. "O, ọmọ mi," she says now, "not everyone needs a reason."

DURING THE DAY, as you answer the phones, listening to customers who want you to solve all their problems, you feel a rippling, like a tiny rat let loose underneath your skin.

The customer on the phone is telling you that his data disappeared immediately after he loaded it. You ask for his details while brushing against the scratch marks Ojukwu made on the inside of your elbow. It tickles, you shudder, swallow back nausea.

"What is the worst thing you've done?" you ask 08056647737, Olajide Benson, of 76A, Eunice Bashorun Street, Victoria Island.

"Like how?" He sounds confused. "With my Glo SIM card?"

"No, in life. What's the worst thing? Are you a wicked person? Have you hit a woman?"

"Is this a survey you are doing?"

"Yes," you lie.

"Well, I don't remember really. I must have done bad things in my childhood, you know? In my youth too. I went to Unilag, I was even in a cult, but that's all in the past. But wo, see, if we really look at it, you'll see that we're all wicked in this country. I'm watching the news now, have you seen that our governor is demolishing innocent poor people's houses just so he can build expensive estates?"

"And do you believe in reincarnation?"

"What?" He sounds panicked now. "Is this Globacom customer care?" He hangs up.

You charge his line a fee for no reason.

◊ ◊ ◊

YOU ANSWER YOUR MOTHER after the thirty-seventh missed call. Your father has sent you *Please, just talk to your mum* texts; *She was wrong, but she's hurting* texts; *Come home, let's talk* texts. Each new one bumps an old one away, all unanswered. Your mother is crying now, saying she is sorry and could you possibly forgive her?

"It's because I heard you humming that song. It was her song. How did you know it?"

"I don't know, Mummy."

". . . and I saw you doing all those things that she would do, and . . ."

And she tells you that all she could see superimposed on

your facial features, so like hers, was her own mother cutting her arms with a razor and stuffing the wound with powdered chile pepper, and her mother locking her out of the house if she played in the street too long, and her mother smashing a full bottle of beer on her father's head so that the musty smell of beer mixed with the sharp smell of blood and both liquids soaked up his Limca T-shirt before he slumped to the ground and died at her feet.

"I've done things too," you say.

"But Jesus can save you!" Your mother says Jesus has saved her, and had you not noticed that she has always been a kind mother to you, and never hit you, or screamed at you? Not until the day she saw her mother reappear on your face and freaked out and reverted to the self her flesh wanted her to be, even though her spirit had overcome through Christ who strengthens her.

You hadn't noticed extreme kindness, but perhaps only because there hadn't been the opposite present to emphasize it. She has been a good mother, a goodness you have taken for granted. Your father has been a good father, if oddly protective of your mother and her extreme religiosity. You are starting to understand that this must stem from knowing her history.

"He can save you!" your mother repeats. "Jesus saves!"

You are sitting in your car outside your friend Fatima's house; she is celebrating a promotion. You yank the rearview mirror down to check your lipstick. A pimple is glowing red.

"Mummy, I have to go."

"Wait, wait! Come with me for deliverance, Pastor Kalejaiye is coming on Sunday. We can get it out of you. Jesus can—"

Fingernails bite into palms. Bite out: "I said I have to go."

◊ ◊ ◊

YOU WALK INTO AN INTERVENTION in Fatima's living room. Six of your friends are there, including Lesley. No Amaka.

Nobody sits next to you on the fuchsia couch.

The last time you were all together, it was your twenty-sixth birthday, and they had surprised you then too, but with a dinner party at Cactus. You remember Fatima had started to make a toast, four glasses of wine in, and said to you, "Babe! Our late twenties are for questioning. Are you who you really want to be? Are you—" and she had hiccupped loudly, a sound that echoed in your head.

You bite the inside of your cheek now, your fists still clenched from the conversation with your mother.

"We know you didn't mean to . . . to hurt the animal. Was it a mistake? You should have just told her instead of running away."

You are quiet, you do not lie to them. Silence becomes your only answer as they go on.

"This is not you," Lesley says. She is standing next to the door as if waiting for a reason to walk out. "I ran into Michael at Chicken Republic the other day and he said you threw water in his face at work? Like, that's so so not you." She looks to someone, anyone else, to support her. They all nod.

"Remember when you flew to Abuja last year just to help me pack?"

"Or when you loaned me fifty thousand naira and refused to take interest?"

"I mean, you convinced your folks to take me in that year in uni after Popsy died."

Their stories do not sound familiar to you at first. Surely

that's not you? The only you to remember is the one that held on tight until Ojukwu stopped breathing. The you that flooded that bathroom without pausing to question your actions. You remember the you that did not flinch when your mother hit you with her Bible—you had stood there, taking it, feeling an awakening within you, a stirring of an animal that had always been there, hibernating, waiting, waiting. But as they keep piling stories on top of each other, the memories melting over your head like cool ice cream, yes, you remember when you slept in the hospital with Tola that weekend, when you sat next to Jude while he came out to his parents, when you loaned Lesley your laptop for her final-year project.

This new horrible person is not you, you start to agree with them, but on the tail of that acknowledgment are doubts in the shapes of laughing hyenas who ask questions like: What about those moments deep within a mundane interaction when you were struck by the realization that your life was a performance? When you were confused about why you were smiling, if you wanted to be smiling, if you were supposed to be smiling, and who your audience was, who you were trying to convince?

If your instinct has always been to suppress the urge to burn the feathers of the gateman's nesting chicken, or to stamp down the itch to run into pedestrians crossing the road, and instead to be there for a friend, to massage your mother's feet, then your friends must be right to believe that's *the real true you*, the one that has prevailed until now.

But then Fatima comes to sit next to you, your body tilting toward hers when the cushion dimples under her weight. She stretches an arm out to you. "We love you," she says, and starts to touch your face, your baby cheeks that know their kisses so well, but she grazes the pimple on your chin and you are fisting up, pulling back, smashing her nose, shouting that she shouldn't touch you.

It is their turn to be silent. Your hand is throbbing in protest. There is blood on your knuckles.

The silence ends as they gather around Fatima, who is screaming, "Fuck-fuck-fuck-izit-broken?"

You stumble through, past them, out of that house that is suffocating you. You want to stay, you want to cry, you want to grovel, you want to believe that the stories they told are real, and all your life has not been acting. That they know you.

◊ ◊ ◊

"I DON'T KNOW that I can overcome this, Mummy," you cry to your mother on the phone, your knuckles still wet with Fatima's blood. "It's inside me." You are so scared that you believe it.

Your mother reminds you that you had always been a sweet child, always smiling at your parents, always making friends, always making them proud, even with your odd habits of plucking out your hair or yanking the tail of the neighbor's cat. But how does she know the hair-plucking and cat-bullying weren't the true parts? The joy at killing weevils? Your mother is sure that this is a result of her mother's blood in you, genetics, but what if the independent you, the distinct you, the *you*-you, has always pined for this cruelty, wanted it, waited on it? She suggests church again. She brings up fasting and prayer.

"Look, Agnes . . . she insisted I call her Agnes . . . she died from a mild fever at twenty-six; what if she's back to finish the work she started in that life? My pastor reminded me that in the Bible, King

Jehoiakim was wicked and started his reign at twenty-five; but King Amaziah also started his reign at twenty-five and he was a good man, a good king! There's no coincidence here. Your spirit wants to choose and we must cast out the spirit of Agnes!" This theory of your mother's appeals to you: It's not your fault.

You tell your mother no, you won't go to her church's deliverance service, you don't believe in that, but yes, you will fast and pray with her if she thinks it will help. Abstaining from food for seven days to purge yourself of this other hunger seems cosmically right to you. You will fast; she will do the praying.

On day one of fasting, twelve customers hang up on you.

On day two of fasting, you call in sick, you spread tea tree oil over your pimples, including the third one. Then the fourth.

On day three of fasting, your mother calls to pray with you, to encourage you. She went through this, she reminds you. After her mother died, she hadn't known how to react. Whether to weep with joy, or with grief. She had gone on a rampage, a decade-long biting phase. She bit from the age of six till she was sixteen. She was the sixteen-year-old with a biting problem. She bit her family members, she bit strangers, she bit herself, enjoyed the taste of skin and sweat in her mouth, between her teeth. But then the Lord had saved her. The pastor's wife took her in at sixteen and introduced her to Jesus.

On day four of fasting, you squeeze pus out of your tenth pimple. Your belly pulls down to meet your spinal cord, your eyes roll back. You bite your tongue until blood pools. You go down to the parking lot of the dingy hotel you're staying at for the duration of the fast. Enter your car. Put the gear in drive and hold your breath until your car rolls into the parked Mercedes-Benz in front of you. Breathe out.

Maybe if you indulge this urge within you, instead of abstaining from it, the pimples will go away, you will exhaust Agnes away. Then you can return to yourself.

So when you slap the security guard at ShopRite, feeling his jaw shift beneath your palm, when you go into the parking lot of the small church, slashing all the tires under the cover of the night and the choir's discordant singing, when you set fire to the makeshift buka at the end of your office street, the one where you've gone to eat amala with your colleagues every Friday, you bite down the thrill, the buzz in your head; you ask yourself, instead, if this will be the last time, if this will be the final act that will release you from Agnes.

◇ ◇ ◇

AT NIGHT, living in your car now because you need the distance from people, you wake up to a heavy smell. A smell of wet dog, animal breath, cat piss. You roll down the windows, but you know it won't go. The smell is coming from you.

◇ ◇ ◇

"IS YOUR MOTHER RUNNING AWAY?" People have asked you this question your whole life—a question the Yoruba ask children who closely resemble their parents—but you have always smiled the polite smile of the good child who is seen but not heard.

You're driving through Alausa, far from any home on this Thursday night. The streets are quiet, save for the sounds of

Afrobeat drums and trumpets from Fela's Afrika Shrine that come to you softly on the breeze. Some schoolgirls were raped in this neighborhood two months ago. You read the news on Twitter and closed the app because: too much evil everywhere. Now the music fuzzes this memory, renders the night elastic, the area spirited.

Do they ask if your mother is running away because you have taken her onto your face, to keep as a memory for when she's gone? Resemblance as memento? Or do they mean that you have trapped your mother, imprisoned her on your face, so she can't run away? So that she can't run away even if she is thinking about it? Because she is thinking about it?

And what do mothers run from?

You are two streets away from the Afrika Shrine now; the music and voices are louder. "Bang! Bang! Bang!" the people sing-shout Femi Kuti's song.

Do mothers run from daughters who remind them that they carry their own mothers on their faces?

"Sister? You wan park?" One of the area boys is flagging you down, directing you to a possible free parking spot. "Sister! Come park here!"

What else is passed along with round cheeks, a wide sweaty nose, brown eyes?

◊ ◊ ◊

ONE DAY, you looked down at your hands in your lap but what you saw were Agnes's hands, ashy and shaky and old and scabbed over from all the violence.

◇ ◇ ◇

"SISTER, YOU DEY GO SHRINE?"

The area boy is now hanging from your window, asking if you are here to join the festivities. His face is shadowed and his features blend into each other in the night. The hunger for the two hundred naira you will slip into his hands if he parks you makes his bloodshot eyes bright. You make out a missing tooth. "Space dey for this corner!"

Don't say a word to him as he guides you into a dark side street, hopping in front of your car, stopping every other moment to make sure you're still there even though your headlights are illuminating him in a glow that seems to beckon you. Maybe this is your own light, like Saul's light in Damascus. The turning point. One big move to expel Agnes.

Answer the beckon. Step on the accelerator. Watch him go down, his hands go up. Listen to the screaming, the crunching, the screaming.

Flick the dead off.

◇ ◇ ◇

EVERYBODY IS CALLING YOU. Lesley is calling you. Fatima is calling you. Your other friends are calling you. Unknown numbers are calling you. Your father is calling you, texting you. Hasn't this gone on long enough? When are you coming home? Won't you forgive your mother's violence? He wants to know why your mother isn't saying anything—just weeping and praying. He wants to know why your friend is calling him saying something about a dog, about a nose?

You twist the rearview mirror of your car so you can stare at your face in the warm glow of a streetlight. There are pimples everywhere. There is one on the very tip of your nose that has changed your face. That tiny bump, among all the others, a result of excess sebum and dead skin cells trapped in the pores of your skin, that tiny bump, has thrown off the balance of your face.

After you drove away—your heart rattling hard, like a secondhand organ, used in another lifetime—after you drove far enough for the tires to stop tracking blood, you listened for the quiet, for the end, for yourself. The rippling beneath your skin is pulling it apart, like stretch marks widening until what is beneath is above. You are choking on your own skunk smell, you stink like burning rubber. There is an emerging. Perhaps all you needed was permission, the excuse of genetics so the real you could manifest. You wanted this, didn't you?

In the mirror, you do not recognize yourself. And it's because there is no you there. Ignore the phone calls. Leave the messages unanswered. There is no you here. There is Agnes.

BREASTMILK

THE WARM, SLIMY CREATURE THAT IS MY SON IS PLACED in my arms. He is crying a grating, lusty soprano. I stretch my mouth into the likeness of a smile. I don't look down at the baby. I hold him loosely: too tight and he might squirt out of my grip and ricochet off the white walls of my hospital room.

"We're going to cut the cord now, mummy," one of the nurses says, and I nod. She says *mummy* in that patronizing tone I use when I tell my cousin's children that they are so big and tall and grown now.

"Can I cut it?" Timi asks.

I don't hear what they say to him, how these efficient women tell him no. But I see him step back, his head lowered as if he's been chastised. I could have told him that this is not one of those New Age hospitals that allow men to actively participate in the birth, that the father is merely a bystander here, a witness. But I didn't. There are many things I don't say to my husband.

The baby is taken from me so he can be cleaned, so I can be cleaned too. Through the haze of twelve-hour labor pains, I watch my husband reach out to receive our baby from the nurse, now swaddled in the ewedu-colored cloth we bought. I am tired.

My gritty eyes want to close against the world, and my aching body wants to gather its leaking, melting shape into itself so I can recover from all the pushing and groaning and bloody catastrophes of childbirth. But I want to watch Timi's first moments of fatherhood. His body is stiff, in the practiced hold they taught us in prenatal classes: baby's neck in the crook of your elbow, the other hand supporting the rest of the weight. He swings his head toward me—the only part of his body he releases from this wooden stance that proclaims fierce responsibility and a dash of pride—and smiles. Through mine, I see the sheen of his tears.

I turn away and settle back into the pillow.

◊ ◊ ◊

IN THE MORNING, my mother shows up. She is telling me that she came as soon as she could, that my father would be proud of this feat of mine, bringing new life into the world. And am I glad? Am I relieved? Am I fine? Am I proud?

I am excused from responding to her barrage because I am a woman who just had a baby, an exhausted woman who endured earth-shifting contractions, who thrashed through a forest of clawing pain, whose pelvic region throbs as if pounded by a pestle. My mother doesn't sit; she hovers above me, tucking a braid away, stroking my cheek.

I roll my eyes. "What of the conference?"

"Bah," she says, waving fingers as if she hadn't spent the last six months putting the event together. "I have a grandchild!"

The headliner of the conference is a friend of hers, a woman who is combining her research on chemosignals at some Netherlands university with knowledge from her grandmother's traditional beliefs and claiming that with practice, we can all smell emotions. When my concern doesn't fade, my mother adds that her assistant is very capable.

A nurse comes to save me from my mother's good-willed pawing.

"Da-Silva?"

Her uniform is so white, her waist so small. She looks like a cardboard cutout, this nurse. She also looks faintly like someone I have seen on Timi's Facebook when I hit "Load More" so that the life he had before me appears in grainy frozen laughter with strangers. Why do some Nigerian hospitals insist on these silly white caps for their nurses? Her cap looks like a diamondless tiara tucked into her afro bun.

"Yes," my mother answers for me. "This is her."

There are many times I wish my mother would be present to speak for me, with her impassioned activist's voice. Like the night Timi confessed his affair, thirty-eight weeks ago. But am I not an adult?

"Your baby is scheduled to receive formula again in thirty minutes," the nurse says, "but I came to see if there are any changes. Any thick liquid? Clear? Yellow?"

As she reaches for the neck of my hospital gown, I catch her wrist. Her face rearranges itself in surprise, and I think she isn't that pretty; her eyes are too close together. "There's no change," I say.

She twists free and brushes the rescued limb against the front of her dress, as if to restore her composure. "Okay, but I still need to take a look, Mrs. Da-Silva—"

"Ms.," my mother corrects. *"Mizzz."*

What does "Mrs." really mean? is a question I grew up hearing my mother pose to people who could only stutter in response.

The nurse's frown deepens; she is unsettled by this interaction with me and my mother. "I'm sorry, *Miz* Da-Silva. Your son isn't pooping as much as we'd like. He's okay, but to be safe, I'm going to have to feel around for colostrum, milk."

That's all I did last night while Timi slept in a chair beside me. I prodded and tugged and massaged, but my breasts have stayed swollen to unfamiliar D-cups, nipples stubbornly dry. They told me milk, or something like it, would come a few months into pregnancy, or around birth.

"I said there's nothing." I jerk the top of the gray sack of a gown they have put me in. I turn away from the nurse's unpretty face to my mother's, which is now contemplating me with a frown.

◊ ◊ ◊

TIMI HOLDS MY HAND, and my mother caresses my shoulder while cradling our baby in one elbow. Another day has passed, and the doctor is asking questions before discharging us. I hang limp in Timi's clasp. His palms are always so dry. How do I trust a man whose sweat glands won't betray him? His palms were dry then too, when he stroked my arm and informed me he was going to Abuja for business, just business. But should this man trust his wife who claims she forgives his affair, who pardons his cheating so easily, a wife who says everything is forgotten and buried? A wife who kisses those dry palms the morning after his confession and says, "We're good, babe." Should he trust this woman if she doesn't believe the truth of her own forgiveness?

I wriggle free from Timi's hold and reach for the baby we have not yet named; we have two more days till the naming ceremony. My mother lowers him into my arms.

"And don't worry about lactating," the doctor is saying. "I don't want you to worry at all. Lactation happens late for some women, others not at all. Some women even say breastfeeding is old-fashioned! But everything is fine as long as baby is loving the delicious formula."

I want to ask the doctor how he knows the formula is delicious, if it is more delicious than breastmilk, if the baby can tell the difference.

When we saw the baby's penis for the first time, pointed out to us in the jumble that is an ultrasound, the nurse gave a practiced chuckle. "See how he's proud of that penis!" she said. Timi's eyes liquefied. I turned away from him and away from my son's penis, to look at the fetal growth chart on the wall. A son? My heart broke a little. A son who could grow up to become a man, a man who might hurt other people no matter how well I raise him because a man is a man, even when he is the best man—as Timi has shown me. I gathered myself and turned back to smile at the monitor.

Maybe it started there, my body's rejection of my child, visiting the sins of father on son?

I lower my head to blow air into my baby's face, my mouth a soft *o*. My smile is not forced when he wrinkles his face and blinks at me.

"If you want to see our lactation consultant," the doctor adds, "you're welcome to do so. He's not in-house, though well recommended. Give it some time, I'd say. Baby is fine, poop is fine, all is fine!" The doctor has three horizontal tribal marks on each cheek that squirm when he speaks. My baby's cheeks look extra smooth in comparison. I press my lips to that smoothness. Timi beams at this picture and asks if I'm ready to go home.

◊ ◊ ◊

ALL OUR FAMILY MEMBERS come out for the naming ceremony. Their voices ring loud as they celebrate me, celebrate
Timi. A first child, a son! Someone has dropped a thick white
envelope into my lap—for my hard work, they say. I let the
insulting thing slide off.

Timi strolls around in his agbada made from the matching
guinea brocade his mother bought for us, a baby-blue shade of
sky we haven't seen since harmattan started. He stops to laugh
at someone's joke, the cloth billowing around him, so natural, so
man, so *Timi*. He has been cradling our baby all day, as if eager to
show off how modern he is, a rare Nigerian man who "allowed"
his wife to keep her mother's name, a man who will be involved
in the care of his child. I want to yank the baby from him, but
I do not have the right. The one bond that ties baby to mother,
at least for the first year, is missing. My breasts oppress me with
their emptiness.

We name him Fikayo; we call him Fi. Olufikayo. All the
names I suggested were Finn, Fenton, Fran, because my love of
F names had lingered from devouring all that angsty British liter-
ature when I was a teenager. But Timi reminded me that we are
Yoruba, not English, and the name should reflect that.

Is there a Yoruba name for "this child was conceived in the
throes of hurt and anger"? An Egun name for "this boy is a result
of your forgiveness sex after your husband confessed his wrong"?

I acquiesced easily to his sensible argument about the names,
remembering how he had quietly rebutted my reservations about
becoming his girlfriend six years ago, an elevation from our
casual fling. "Come on, we have the same views on the important

things, Aduke!" he said. "That's what's important ni t'ori Qlqrun. That's a foundation not many folks have."

Timi's mother's pastor calls out the names, Olufikayo Olujimi Olatunde. The people cheer and toast with glasses of wine and zobo under the canopy we rented for the day. When the robed pastor dabs anointing oil on Fikayo's head, the baby begins to cry. I jump up to snatch him.

"He's hungry," I murmur to no one in particular, and retreat into the house. I hear music pick up behind me, Sunny Ade blasting from rented speakers, my cousin's children screaming at each other, Timi's mother shouting for the caterer to start serving small chops. The woman's Christian benevolence is what prevents friction between her and my mother, between me and her, between her and Timi. "Love thy neighbor as thyself," she mutters to herself frequently, like a calming mantra, shrugging in acceptance even when she doesn't understand why her son is acting "like a woman," doing household chores and sharing the financial decision-making with me. The microphone screeches and I close the nursery door behind me, but the door is not thick enough to drown them out.

One of my aunties has tied my iro for me, insisting that the tighter the wrapper, the faster my pregnancy pouch will shrink. I release my belly now and flop down into the armchair. I shift Fi in my arms and draw the diaper bag closer with a foot. It is an awkward process; I haven't yet perfected the juggling acts of motherhood.

He quiets when the nib fills his mouth, and I am envious of a plastic bottle.

My aunt finds me dozing off while Fi feeds.

"Ahn ahn, feeding bottle kẹ?" Her gele is maroon and silver, and the light from the window reflects against the scaly material. I squint and look down at Fi. He has fallen asleep.

"Auntie," I say.

"But kilode? Why are you not breastfeeding, mgbọ?" She crosses her arms under her own breasts. "Deyemi's wife had the nerve to tell me she was not breastfeeding so her breasts won't sag. Sag! You too, Aduke? Does your mother know about this decision?"

"Auntie, auntie!" I check to make sure Fi is still sleeping and lower my voice. "There's no milk, auntie." I have begun to cry.

My aunt's face relaxes. She moves to pick Fi up, places him in his cot. She leans forward then, as if to hug me.

"I know what to do. Jumoke had this same problem, but you should see her now! The baby girl is three, and we're begging her to stop. I will send you one agbo that my sister makes in Ijebu. You will rub it like . . ." She reaches for my breasts, through the baby-blue brocade, through my bra, and begins to knead. I feel myself leaving my body through a frustrated sigh, floating to the ceiling of the lilac nursery with the white silhouettes, above my own gele, above my auntie's gele, which dips forward in rhythm with her hands, above my body, above my shame.

◊ ◊ ◊

OUR FRIENDS VISIT WITH GIFTS that are not newborn-baby appropriate. Only Sandra, who writes an annoyingly whole-some mummy blog with a large readership, shows up without a hard-edged toy, but she also brings along a pious look to throw at the feeding bottle and formulas. If I were to check, I would probably find an irate blog post railing against them. When he catches the glance, Timi tells Sandra that I need to rest. The others bring laughter and warmth and kisses for Fi, but I am grateful when I walk the last person out the front door and return to the silence of our living room. Timi is sitting on the edge of an armchair, and I know he wants to speak with me. I grab a bib from the floor and head to the nursery, to my baby, to hide.

"Aduke."

I turn to look at my husband, his wide nose, the Cupid's bow that would fight Rihanna's for perfection. The first time I kissed him, I let my tongue trace that dip, recarving it with my lust.

"Are you okay?" he asks now.

"Yeah, why?"

"You've been kind of distant."

What I should say is: I don't care about your stupid ex; I care that I don't know how to be angry about her. What I say instead is: "We just had a baby, Timi. Have you read any of Sandra's articles about motherhood?" The laugh that punctuates my sentence is a weak sputter.

Timi points at me, then at himself. "We're okay?" He wants my eyes to meet his; I hear it in his question. They meet. Mine skitter away.

"We're great," I say. I look down to find my baby's bib crumpled in my fist. I straighten out the butterflies on soft white cotton, blue and orange and pink. "I'm just tired, you know?"

"But you—"

I look up, afraid he will say that I am not even breastfeeding, that he will ask me what is making me tired.

"You don't even let me help with Fikayo. You're always sleeping in the damn nursery. This wasn't our plan o, Aduke."

Of course, Timi is not insensitive. He rises right along with me when Fi cries us awake. I keep shushing him away, back to sleep, away from the nursery.

"I just feel a bit guilty about the breastmilk thing. Maybe I'm overcompensating." I push the fiction out of my lungs easily.

Back in Sunday school, where my mother used to send me before she decided religion hated women, the teacher would pipe, "To err is human; to forgive, divine," even if we kids didn't know what it meant to err. Now that Timi has shown me what it means, the homily taunts me. If to forgive is divine, why am I resisting my own divinity? I want to feel the righteousness that comes with forgiving infidelity, but all I feel is shame at my lack of backbone, my lack of indignation, and fear that if it happens again, I will just as easily forgive Timi.

My husband is good, has been good. This was a fluke, and he confessed immediately because he knew I would want to know immediately, and he was sorry, and he is sorry every day, and I could see him hurting because he knew he had hurt me, and he is so very sorry, sorry in a way that I believe?

Am I even my mother's daughter, to be thinking about forgiveness?

Now Timi is asking if I think this is postpartum depression.

"I'm not depressed. Just tired."

"Come back to bed," he begs. "I miss you."

I flinch.

"God, I'm not talking about sex. I'm not a monster!"

I raise both hands in surrender. "Yeah, we can move his cot to our room tomorrow. How about that?"

When Timi lets out a dissatisfied breath, covering his face, its beautiful features, with his hands, I flee into the nursery, closing the door that is only wood, not metal, not thick enough to protect me. But why do I need protection? Why shouldn't *he* be seeking protection from *me*? I want to be the type of woman who would have turned into a pillar of flames when Timi told me about sex with the ex in Abuja. I want to have singed the confession off his tongue until the smell of his own burning choked him, robbing him of oxygen till he was flat on his face, at my feet, melting in my fury. I want to be a woman like my mother. There are You-Tube videos of my mother cutting down the governor at a rally organized by her nonprofit for women's development. The governor had said she should leave politics to men. "Don't you dare, Mr. Olusegun Adetula!" my mother screamed, spittle gathering in the corner of her Ruby Woo-painted lips. "Don't you dare belittle the women who carry this society. We carry it!" But no, I went straight into his arms. Mine was a faltering anger: here, then gone. My mother would be disgusted to see the weakness in her spawn.

◊ ◊ ◊

WE'RE IN THE NURSERY. I am seated on the floor between my mother's knees on a folded blanket, feeding Fikayo while my mother lines my scalp with oil. The smell of the coconut oil meets the smell of formula in my nostrils. Fi is naked against my bare breasts, skin-to-skin bonding my mother scoffed at the first time she saw us in this position. "Bonding?" She laughed. "Where did you read about this one now?" But this proximity to his sucking mouth, even if the milk doesn't come, has me flushed with feeling. Fi tugs on the bottle against my breasts while my mother tugs softly at my hair, plaiting straight cornrows. This is what it is like to be a mother and a daughter.

Timi is cooking okra soup in the kitchen, and when a waft strays into the room, I hear my mother's belly rumble. We laugh. A husband who shares the kitchen with me is something I am proud of, a way of life my mother approves of, preaches. She works through a tangled section, and I stiffen my neck in discomfort.

"Sorry, does it hurt?"

I shake my head.

"How's the copywriting?"

"Fine. I submitted June's calendar yesterday."

"It's stupid they didn't give you time off."

"It's fine. If I stop, they'll find some mass comm student to do it for cheaper. It's just words; I can handle it."

"And Timi's work?"

"Good. He's building a website for Coke with Deji."

"And"—she continues to plait my hair—"are the two of you okay?"

I take a deep breath and try to relax my shoulders so my mother doesn't sense the tension this question elicits. "Why?"

I feel her shrug. I wonder if she has somehow smelled the strain through my scalp. Maybe her professor friend has taught her nose a trick or two. And if so, what emotion is she identifying? Shame? Resentment? Anger? How do I tell my mother, the woman who told me never to stay with a man who disrespects me in any way, that I am doing just that? That not only did Timi disrespect me with this affair, but I couldn't even flare up in response?

Whenever we heard a story of a husband who left, who hit, who had another family in a village somewhere, my mother would joke that my father—"that one who died to escape my wahala"— knew dying was better than misbehaving. That he knew she wouldn't have stayed a minute longer, that her blood was thicker than that. He had met her on the streets of Unilag waving a placard that read WOMEN ARE STUDENTS TOO! STUDENTS, NOT MAIDS! STUDENTS, NOT SEX OBJECTS! He joined the protest that day, later finding out she was the last daughter from a polygamous family she never completely forgave for their lack of attention. "That's your mama's origin story," he used to say to me when I sat on his lap and pulled at his full beard, "our superhero." Joking about my father's death made me squirm, even though I recognized the dark humor as the coping mechanism it was. But she would look at me with those blazing eyes that want all the good in the world for me and say, "Women suffer enough. Don't add man problem on top. Keep your shoes beside the door."

I can't tell her now that maybe her superior blood thinned with me.

"We're fine," I say. But I have waited too long. She knows I am hedging.

She will not push it, though. Instead, she will scoot her chair away from the table later at dinner, announcing her departure, leaving a full bowl of delicious food untouched, leaving Timi thinking that he has offended her with too much salt. But I will know it is my mother bringing her protests from the streets of Lagos into my home.

◊ ◊ ◊

MY MOTHER IS GONE and Timi wants to talk again; he wants to hammer this out once and for all. He wants to be sure we are good, are we good, are we good, are-we-good-arewegood? Timi wants to know, Timi wants.

I walk into our bedroom where we have moved the cot, away

from Timi's questioning voice. I want to look down into my baby's
face with his always-puckered brows, to have his lustrous brown
eyes look back into mine, his chubby puff-puff cheeks reassure me
with their fullness, his plastered curls remind me of newness and
freshness and growth.

Instead I find my baby turning blue in the face. His fingers are
fisted tight; his arms are flailing little sticks. Has the strain hanging in the air of our bedroom asphyxiated our son?

◊ ◊ ◊

WHEN THE DOCTOR TELLS ME that Fikayo has a gastroesoph-
ageal reflux, an allergic reaction to the formula, that breastmilk
would be ideal at this point, I feel a sharp pain in my breasts.
Can guilt be felt physically, like a blade on a finger, like a cramp
in the calf, like biting your own tongue?

◊ ◊ ◊

THE LACTATION CONSULTANT'S OFFICE is in the Boys'
Quarters. We squeeze past two jeeps in the narrow driveway to
get to the one-room office at the back of the main house. The
signage is lopsided, dusty, but my doctor said Dr. Laoye is good
at what he does.

Timi and I sit on the couch while he paces.

"Have you taken any cod-liver oil?" he asks after I tell our
story, that a fourth formula is being tested on Fi, that my baby is
now bones in a bag of soft skin, that my auntie's agbo didn't work.

I shake my head.

Dr. Laoye reminds me of those boys I loved when I was thirteen. The older boys in our estate who looked big and tall and bounced with a swagger to buy Guinness from the shop where I would be buying matches or Maggi or cotton wool. They looked like the epitome of adulthood to me with their loud, uncontained laughter and colorful rubber wristbands, as if they knew exactly what they wanted and how to get it: beer, life.

And that had been Timi too, so dogged in his pursuit of me, his want of me. What fractured this want, insinuated a pause long enough for Abuja to happen?

"This isn't about you," is what my mother might say in this situation, as she has done before, those days I came home crying about a boy who didn't love me back, a friend who stopped talking to me, a job I didn't get. How she would straighten my shoulders and wipe my face and insist, "It isn't about you. Roll it off. Those who appreciate you will come." How she would embrace me, "my gentle, sensitive baby" whispered into my hair in a voice I thought sounded mournful or scared, and I would go back into the world trying to be less gentle, bolder, demanding more from life once I saw things through the filter of my mother's opinions.

Dr. Laoye asks me to sit on the consultation chair and take off my blouse and bra. I like that he has not looked to Timi for permission or acknowledgment, unlike many nurses at the hospital who ask about my husband before attending to me.

I look nowhere as the cool from the air conditioner tightens my now-bare nipples. Not at Timi, not at the doctor. I pin my arms down, fighting the urge to cover myself.

Dr. Laoye peers at my breasts, then cups them in his gloved hands, latex against breasts.

This is the first time a man has touched my breasts since the night of confession. That night with Timi that brought us Fi, that angry night when I allowed my nails to dig into his back, scratch at his skin, draw blood, when he held my breasts and bit them, and I arched into the violence of his mouth, asking him to press down harder, longer, forever.

Could my confused pleasure of that night have ruined me for my child?

The doctor squeezes gel into his palm and gets to work on my breasts. The gloves glide over my skin with the slippery, tingly gel, with a soft sound, his fingers moving first in an elliptical motion from the sternum, round and round, till he tugs at the nipples.

As the tugs become harder, I hunch over. Dr. Laoye lightly grazes my shoulder, tender, an unspoken *relax*. My eyes shoot up to find Timi's. His face is blank, too straight, and I know he is struggling to show me nothing.

I think: Look at another man touching me, Timi.

And then I feel it, a warm trickle out of my left nipple. The milk feels like a living creature crawling out of me. I look down at my chest, then up to share this moment with Timi, but he has turned away.

◊ ◊ ◊

THE HOSPITAL WANTS TO TEST my breastmilk before they introduce it to Fi. *My* breastmilk. Fi's. Even while the doctor explains milk content to me, why they are testing, how the mother passes on more than fat and protein, how toxicity the mother has been exposed to can be a risk to the baby, all I can hear is *your* breastmilk. Timi's gaze keeps drifting down to my unbound breasts under the boubou.

Later, my mother shows up at the hospital with the woman

from her conference, the smell professor. The woman has decided to take up a visiting professorship from Unilag, and they have just come back from lunch. I reach for my mother's hands. "We're waiting to hear," I say.

"Timi?" I can see my mother's nose wrinkle when she says his name. I will not confirm her suspicions.

"With Fi," I reply.

Another nurse comes to stand by the bed. "It's time to pump again, madam."

The nurse pulls apart the flaps of the hospital gown and starts to apply lubrication to my nipples. I do not move to help. I do not move away. I just lie there, a body. When the pump has been attached and turned on, my mother's professor friend stands to leave the room. The swish of her colorful kimono disappears around the door. My mother goes out after her.

I am now alone with the nurse, who is intently watching the liquid stream down the tubes into the bottle. *What are you looking for?* I want to ask. This feeling of milk out of my breasts is so strange, as if a string were being unspooled out and out and out. *What can you see?*

◊ ◊ ◊

WHEN I STIR FROM SLEEP, my mother and her professor friend have returned to the room. My mother rushes to fuss over me.

"Mummy," I say, shifting my face away from her pesky touches. "Do you want to check on Timi and Fi?"

"Yes, yes." She hurries out of the room, happy to be useful, leaving me with the professor.

"Good evening," I whisper, remembering my manners. She

turns toward me. Her face looks sunken, the wrinkles fanned around like the lines on a palm to be read. She nods at my greeting and walks closer to the bed, almost regal in carriage. She stops before she reaches me.

I am curious: What is it about me that is repellent to her? Why won't she come closer? Can her trained nose smell my shame? My failing motherhood, wifehood? My failed daughterhood, too?

She is quiet for so long that I think she has not heard. But then she takes two steps closer. When she speaks, her accent is a flavored reflection of all the places she has lived, nasal and clipped and flat and lyrical all at once. "Good evening." She shifts. "What is it?"

I am not surprised at her question. "What can you smell?" I ask, doing the Nigerian thing of responding to a question with another.

She laughs, but her face is sad. "Darling," she says, and this endearment, which I would find annoying coming from anyone else, fits. "But darling, you smell a lot like your mother."

◊ ◊ ◊

MY MOTHER WALKS HER FRIEND out to get a taxi, and I slip out of bed. I move down the corridor, climb the flight of stairs that will bring me to my baby's ward. I find Timi asleep on a chair next to Fi's cot, a thin curtain their only privacy from the rest of the room. I stand there staring at my family.

"Timi," I whisper, and he jerks awake.

"Hey," he says, rubbing his eyes. He looks at my breasts, and

I follow his gaze. There are splotches where milk has leaked onto my gown.

"Timi," I say again.

He stands and leads me out of the ward to the dim corridor. A fluorescent light farther down blinks every few seconds.

"Hey, what's wrong?" His hands rest on my shoulders. He runs them down my arms, slides them back up.

"I've forgiven you," I say. For my job, I rely on the thesaurus, finding new ways to say old things, fancy ways to turn the client's directives into copy the consumers can relate to. But for my own life, the words are flat. I can say only what I can say.

He becomes still. He swallows. "You said you had."

"I have. I swear." I raise my hands to trap his on my shoulders. While my belly swelled with our baby, I would smile at my beautiful husband, who was the first man I felt confident enough about to introduce to my mother, a man I was sure wouldn't misbehave. Surely I must have suckled some fire from my own mother's breasts, even if just a trace. I press down on Timi. Hard. "I just hate that it was so easy."

I feel him go rigid. This is the first time I am allowing us to discuss the affair since he dropped that suitcase and knelt in front of me, crying, begging for forgiveness. "What are you saying, Aduke?"

There is a scar on Timi's chin, a small diagonal line hidden mostly by his beard, and I like to rub my thumb against the slight elevation. He says he doesn't know how it got there. But what would the scar say if it could speak? If the body could tell what it doesn't forget, doesn't process? I reach out to touch it now.

"I'm saying I am angry that it was so easy," I tell him. "I needed to say that to you."

The doctor says toxicity passes unto the child through breast-milk. If I don't tell Timi these things, will my fluids flood with unvocalized coarse emotions? Will I choke my son with the force of them?

My hands fall to my side; I release Timi. He drops to a squat. He is trembling; he holds his face. "Give me something to do. Give me a list, anything. What can I do?" His voice thickens. "What can I do?" He loses balance and latches onto my knee. I look down at my husband's head. There isn't anything he can do differently. This is about me, was always about me.

The fluorescent bulb flickers again, like a flashlight panning an abandoned room, lighting up things that have stayed in the dark too long.

◊ ◊ ◊

THE NEXT MORNING, my milk is declared safe for Fi by the doctor with the tribal marks. He smiles wide, all those scarred commas stretching.

When Fi is placed into my arms, when his lips and gums circle and clamp onto my nipple, I cannot stop crying. Emotion rises up my chest, hot and forceful, up my neck, up my head, then crashes over me. I pull him closer to my heavy breasts. I hold him tight. My wet kisses slobber all over his forehead. Does that nose look like mine? Those eyes, like my mother's? "My sweet baby," I cry. "I love you," I weep. "I love you," I sob.

My mother sits by my head, letting me cry, stroking my braids. Timi shows up just outside the door, keeping his distance, still reeling from yesterday's talk. My mother stops stroking. She stands up, beams at me, says, "Look, my baby is a mother. Her own woman." Her voice is gentle—no mourning, no concern, no fear.

I nod at Timi to come closer, and he stumbles across the threshold to join my mother and me, my baby and me.

CONTRIBUTIONS

WE HAVE BEEN PRACTICING ESUSU FOR A LONG TIME.
Our mothers did it, our mothers' mothers did it. And probably
their own mothers, too. We've never had a problem of this kind
before, nothing so significant before this woman showed up.
Nothing we couldn't fix, anyway.

This is how our system works: Each woman has one month
to contribute a certain amount of naira. Our names are on a list,
and when that month is over, whoever's number one takes it all.
Then the contributions begin again, and at the end of the second
month, number two collects. The names are always in random
order. We go down the list until the last person has collected, then
reset. This works for us. We don't need your banks; we don't need
your loans. We can take care of ourselves.

Things aren't always smooth. There was the time Iya Ibeji
wasted her collection on a trip to Dubai—camel rides and
shopping—and then couldn't make her contribution the next
month. We had to seize her frozen food store's generator until she
came up with the money. We are not wicked people, you must
understand, but for this system to work, there has to be order.
Another time, Mrs. B had to pay hospital bills for her son's oper-

ation. If we show pity even once, our structure will collapse on itself, so we seized Mrs. B's daughter. The daughter made meals for us, she carried our bags when we went to the market, relieving us of some burdens; she rubbed our feet and plaited our hair. When Mrs. B raised the money, we sent her daughter back home. We still have fond memories of the girl: her sweet face, her spicy beef stew, the way she sprang, lightly, from foot to foot as if her bones were made of paper.

Ours is a small group. We must be, for trust, for reliability. Not just anyone will accept our terms of admittance, both lifelong and strict. We take what we can until your obligations are met, and for many, this is too much power, too much risk. We haven't invited you here, we tell the ones who balk at our terms, their heads tilted at beseeching angles; go try your luck at the banks. We've worked too hard to allow any stupid leniency that could risk sending us back to the gutters.

So, when the new woman came sniffing at our meeting with her long nose, we warned her, we asked if she was certain. Yes, she said, she needed an alternative to the banks; yes, she said, she was sure. She was a cousin to one of our brothers' best friends, so we said okay, even if we were hesitant—our hands fiddling with wrappers, our chests tight, we welcomed her.

At first, things went smoothly. Nonsense hardly ever shows itself immediately. She paid her contributions on time; she came to the meetings and drank Fanta and ate chin-chin with us. She weighed in on decisions like what color to wear to Sisi Oge's daughter's wedding (pink or burgundy), and whether we should collectively stop patronizing Nature's Way Spa because the owner elbowed one of us on the way to get communion at church. But by the fourth month, she started leaving texts on our phones, begging for more time.

Look, it doesn't work this way.

We appraised her life, checking for what we could seize, what we could take from her so she would understand the gravity of this commitment. We found nothing except a husband and an old mother in the village.

We seized the husband.

Alas, he was useless around our homes. He sat with our husbands, his big beer belly and their big beer bellies all shuddering gelatinously in mirth at some distasteful joke. Her husband screamed at football games with ours, played table tennis in our gardens, whooping like a fool whenever the ball thwacked against the paddle in his hand. Sometimes he looked at us. He looked at us and reminded us of the expanse of our hips, the heft of our breasts; reminded us of the ways our bodies take up space.

We returned the husband, and still she couldn't pay her contribution, so we seized her mother.

Her mother was no better. The old woman sat brooding in corners, her eyes bulging out at us as we picked beans or sewed a button on. She blended in with the cobwebs, her skin acquiring a dark fuzz, a gleaming scaliness, exploiting the shifting shadows. And when she eventually turned into a frog and then a lizard and then a cat, our children squealed in delight. But when they tried to pet the cat, she scratched their hands, drawing blood, leaving scars in the shapes of a strange language. She leapt away from our punishing arms to perch high above our heads, and we craned our necks to look at her, envying the fluffy agility, the way she could wrangle her body into a smaller, lighter version of itself, stealthy and wily and out of reach.

We sent the mother away and called the woman in. What else could she give us to hold on to, until she could make her contribution? We sat her in the center of the group so she could feel our glares prick her skin from every direction, feel the pressure of our disappointment.

Look, she said, will you take my arms?

Her arms were long and muscular and had known work. We accepted them.

They were useful in our kitchens, these arms, chopping ugu leaves here and stirring a pot of ewedu there, pounding yam, slicing apples. They were useful in the household, sweeping dust down the corridor and rocking a child to sleep. Sometimes the arms wrapped around us when our husbands were yelling, or when the children were crying again, or when the sky looked the wrong shade of blue.

But still, she couldn't make her contributions, so we held on to her arms.

My legs? she asked, when—the next month—she still couldn't pay. She sat, armless, collapsed buba sleeves at her sides, in the middle of the circle, her head bowed so that her braids hid her face from our questioning eyes. We had never seen such ineptitude before, such resignation to humiliation. But her legs were sturdy, with firm calves that could kick a football with our sons, and strong knees that braced our daughters' heads when we plaited their hair, and a lap that received our heads when we wept because the sky was still the wrong shade of blue and our eyeballs felt heavy in our heads.

My torso? she offered.

My head? she contributed.

Her voice got airier with each new part given.

And what use were these breasts, this stomach, this heavy head filled with skull? But we took and we took and we took.

It wasn't until we had all her body parts that we saw what she had done.

Had we, too, not always wanted to shed our parts, be lighter, be nothing, be free?

Would we also not give anything to have our bodies no longer belong to us?

Now, we do not speak about it because we are too ashamed to acknowledge how she deceived us into carrying her, bearing her weight forever, her sinew and bones and teeth and muscle and breath and blood. We avoid each other's eyes as we discuss contributions and collections. When we shuffle out of meetings, our shoulders hunch, our treads drag from the burden of her, from carrying what we have taken.

THE HOLLOW

THE HOUSE IS UGLY, ARIT DECIDES WHEN THE TAXI drops her off in front of her new assignment: too many roofs clambering over each other like crowded teeth, and flaking walls the pink of a tongue. She shrugs her tote bag higher and knocks on a gate so black she checks her knuckles for soot. A young boy, maybe fifteen or sixteen, opens to the sound.

She is from the architecture firm, she explains, here to measure for the renovations, and is Madam Oni available?

He waves her in. Madam Oni isn't home, but Arit can proceed with her tasks. His name is Lucky, and he is happy to help if she needs more hands.

She nods, and he retreats to the backyard, leaving her alone. She scratches at the inside of a wrist.

Arit faces the house, and the house faces her. She loosens another shirt button. Even the breeze is balmy, a warm exhalation. She crosses the compound, surveying, analyzing. An overgrown garden a strange tint of green and a gaping carport with no cars, gravel that scatters under her tennis shoes and fences that loom too high, lean too close to the two-level building. Her brain is already simmering with solutions, although she will not design this remodel. She is new at the firm, one year out of university, which means she will be doing the grunt work—measuring, measuring, measuring—until she earns trust. She slings the office camera around her neck, clips the measuring tape at her waist.

What is a house? What do we want from it? What makes it beautiful? Arit's uncle, the man who wooed her to architecture, told her that only when she could answer these questions for herself and for her client should she take pencil to paper. The front door opens at her touch, and she enters, looking.

◊ ◊ ◊

A LONG TIME AGO, there was a woman who lived elsewhere in the city. What is a house—this woman wondered, as her husband dragged her body, like a mop, over faded linoleum floors—but a pressure cooker, a vent pipe screaming steam?

◊ ◊ ◊

ARIT STARTS BY RE-CREATING the ground-floor plan on paper. Her strokes are precise and sure. Little arcs for doorways, short slashes lancing them. Two lines for a wall, another between for a window. There is power in drawing a line into existence, and Arit is deliberate with it, careful.

The interior is cool, and as she moves from room to room, extending her diagram, the sweat on her skin evaporates, leaving a chill. It is a still, contained coolness, one that smells of air that is trapped, waiting. She can neither hear nor see an air conditioner.

She pushes curtains apart. The light seems to hesitate at first, but then it floods in, glancing off the surfaces, filling the spaces, revealing the house to her.

Arit believes that buildings are among the most objective expressions of history. She notes the carpet—gray, vaporous—paws it with a foot to confirm its solidity. The walls: stucco on concrete, a beige that hides dust. She places a palm flat against a wall, the texture tickles. Her hand comes away moist. The curtains: brown, patterned, the kind that were ever present in Nigerian movies of the nineties. The windows live in recesses: narrow, arched, paired up. Furniture is standard family fare: two sofas, two armchairs, one coffee table. There are no paintings, no photographs.

The logic of the layout is lost to her. She turns a bend, expecting to find a room, but no, it is another lonesome nook hosting two cloudy windows. That explains all the roofs. She retraces her steps, and here she is in a guest room, sheets taut on a double bed. Back she goes, and she is in the kitchen now, long and slim with dull beige tiles. The counters are black marble with whorls of white, coiling smoke in a dark night.

Tired, she leans against the sink and looks out to a gnarly backyard—high grass and naked trees. Her drawings make no sense. The walls do not meet on the page, the lines dangle and hang. The house resists containment.

"Well, what do you think of this house of mine?" Madam Oni asks, materializing just inside the back door, a bag of vegetables in hand. Arit reels. The woman has asked her question with urgency or annoyance, as if for the fourth time. Her hair is graying and cut close to her scalp. Her skin is dark, shining, smooth, save for a forehead that furrows and cheeks that sag. Her eyes are narrow, ellipses of bright white punctuating her face. Somewhere in her fifties or sixties, not much taller than five feet.

"I am confused," Arit says, honesty overwhelming professionalism.

Madam Oni snaps, "What were you expecting? Something straightforward?" Arit has no answer. "Can you fix it?" Madam Oni's voice has softened, almost beseeching. "Can you fix it?"

A professor once said that a successful renovation must allow the legacy of the original to shimmer through, to carry forward; and Arit is wary of the hardness of the word *fix*, the incisions of the *x*. She shakes her head. "That's above my pay grade, ma. I'm just here to measure for the as-built drawings. My supervisors will then discuss any solutions with you."

Madam Oni lifts the bag to the counter, turning her back. "Can I have the kitchen for thirty minutes? Lucky, the gate boy, can help you." Her tone is cool again. Arit is dismissed.

"From the relics of household stuff," Honoré de Balzac wrote, "we can imagine its owners in their habitat as they lived"; but as Arit glances at her watch, she sees that three hours of her life have evaporated in this house, and all she can imagine is that no one could live here. She senses an absence, an omission—familiar somehow. Madam Oni, too, seems exhausted, shoulders hunched, head hanging. Arit apologizes and brushes past her client to work outside.

What is a house?

During the evenings Arit's parents worked at their struggling supermarket, her uncle would watch her, and his favorite bonding activity was an architecture lesson. A roof? Floors? Walls? Arit would venture, always logical. But every answer she gave was wrong. No, he would say, try again.

◊ ◊ ◊

THE WOMAN WHO LIVED in a pressure cooker had married a man who waited to reveal the evil festering in his guts. It oozed forth after a few years of marriage, in the form of mistresses, gifts bought for them with the woman's money, as fists to her cheekbones, a foot in her belly, full pots of soup flung at walls, okra sliding down like tears, doors locking her out after trips to the market, doors splintered in the middle of the night.

This woman had a son, and as she stowed him away in cupboards to save him from his father's cruelty, under beds, behind chairs, she wondered, What is a house but a large handbag with many hidden zippers and pockets?

◊ ◊ ◊

ARIT'S CLASSMATES HADN'T UNDERSTOOD why her ambitions didn't go beyond houses. As they aspired to design government buildings and malls and banks and museums and memorials and schools and hotels, cantilevered inventions of steel, muted cubes of concrete, sloping facades of timber, otherworldly curves of glass fiber, Arit had drawn houses: floor plans, exterior elevations, mechanical, electrical, plumbing. She didn't care about schools of style, she cared about unity, about a calming cohesion. She sketched on the blank pages of her novels, between chapters, her dreams filled with sectional 1:20 door and roof details.

The house is the square root of all architecture, her uncle told her. But Arit told peers that her obsession was more about growing up in flats with no storage and shoddy workmanship, with damp windowsills that sprouted mushrooms, with wall edges that left scratches. She quoted their oldest lecturer back to them—over time, bad environments can induce bad mental health—and they accepted her explanation as truth, though she wouldn't meet their eyes. They identified with it.

◇ ◇ ◇

FROM THE OUTSIDE, Madam Oni's house is comprehensible. With Lucky eagerly holding one end of the measuring tape, Arit's site plan and perimeter measurements come together in little more than an hour. She looks up at the house again. The pointed arches of the windows would be better suited to a church, a sanctuary, a building that evil skirts around, passes over.

On the inside, Madam Oni has disappeared, and Arit's calculations still don't add up. She checks and rechecks lengths and widths and heights and never gets the same reading twice. The tape retracts into itself and bites her fingers, again and again. This uncertainty, this shiftiness, this impossibility, causes a ringing in her head. Unmoored, dizzy, she feels as if the walls are the floor and she is leaning against the ceiling, her torso wedged into a window frame. A fear clunks up her ribs, puncturing her breaths, a fear that nothing is real and everything is upside down and elementally wrong. She turns into another lonely corner, seeking a way out, and the sun is streaming through two slender panes, lighting up the carpet, a holy burning.

What does it mean for a house to be fixed? Arit wonders. *To make firm, stable, or stationary // to repair // to set in order or in good condition // to put in a position to make no further trouble // to get even with or revenge upon // to kill, harden, and preserve for microscopic study . . .*

Madam Oni reappears and guides Arit to a chair, a warm hand on her elbow. They take a few steps, or they cross several rooms. The woman pushes a plate of Cabin biscuits and a cup of warm Milo to her. Arit, who associates these with her childhood and rain, looks out to see that, yes, it is indeed raining, and she blinks repeatedly, reminding herself that she is not fourteen and she is an adult and she is safe.

◊ ◊ ◊

THE WOMAN WHO LIVED in the large handbag with many pockets made a plan. She sold aso-ebi from a tiny shop in Balogun Market, saving all the profits, every tip. She sold zobo at church events and ofada rice at community gatherings, the sun darkening her skin, firewood smoke staining her lungs. She opened a bank account, hid the multiplying money from her husband, whose character grew weaker, and the power in his swings, in his words, stronger.

She bought land in a part of Lagos that wouldn't become popular for another eighteen years, a part she had to access on foot because the closest bus stop was twenty minutes away. She hired an eager draftsman who advertised his services in colorful letters under bridges, in scratches on the battered hoods of danfos. And when it was time to build, she oversaw the project herself, breathing her fear into the foundation, sweating her resolve into the concrete walls. She rinsed herself at the site so her husband wouldn't smell new beginnings on her. *Soon, no more,* she chanted in her head every night he added a scar to her skin, every night she added a terrified scream to her son's memory.

When the last shingle was nailed to the roof, the woman put

her son on her back and left, taking nothing else. That first night, they slept on the bare floor, burrowing into each other. A house is freedom, a house is an escape. This one sensed their dread, their relief, and stood vigilant, ready to protect.

◊ ◊ ◊

HOW CAN YOU KNOW a house if you don't sleep in it? Some say that light is the success of any building, but what new angles might darkness reveal?

The last evening Arit spent with her uncle, he took the pencil from her hand, shading dark the windows on the front elevation, shuttering the paper house they'd designed together. "It's nighttime for our inhabitants," he intoned in a cartoony voice, and Arit laughed, enjoying this effort of imagination, the breadth of it.

◊ ◊ ◊

WHEN SHE WAKES IN Madam Oni's house, it is still raining and—according to her watch—well past midnight. She is lying on the couch, warm and protected in its embrace. The half-drunk cup of Milo is on the low table before her, biscuit crumbs glittering on the plate. Madam Oni is asleep in an armchair, her head nestled on her shoulder. Even in sleep, her eyebrows are pinched— anxious, guarded. The only light in the room is from the outside lamps, glowing up the thundering rain, turning the water to sparks.

This is unprofessional, Arit thinks, staying so late in a client's house. Why didn't the woman rouse her, ask her to leave? She wonders if she should be afraid of Madam Oni, but decides no. Her skin doesn't prickle; she senses no terror.

She stands to find a bathroom and shuffles around until she is guided to the foot of the stairs. Though she technically has permission to access the entirety of the house, to complete her measurements, she hesitates. Because the sleeping woman is unable to stop her, Arit feels she's crossing a boundary. But then she notices her left wrist, jittering against her thigh. She climbs.

Nothing creaks as she moves through Madam Oni's house, nothing betrays her; and in this silence, her attention returns to her wrist, to the pulse ticktocking under thin skin. No door opens to a bathroom. Instead, she finds two small bedrooms, one with slippers peeking from beneath a wardrobe, the other with no furniture but an old-fashioned stool, its three legs carved of a rough wood. At the end of a hallway, past an empty lounge, is what must be the master bedroom: a king-size bed, a mattress with no sheets.

As she steps in, the stillness intensifies, breaks across her face like cobwebs. Not a serene calmness, but a muzzled nothingness. Like a familiar hand across a mouth.

◊ ◊ ◊

THE WOMAN WHO LIVED in the house of freedom was found by her husband. On that lot so far away from everything, he climbed the gate, breaching the perimeter, cutting his shin, trailing blood across the compound. He broke a lock, nothing but death swelling in his chest, coating his throat.

The house bristled defensively around the sleeping mother and son, inhaling and exhaling, and the man felt the draft on his neck, on the meat of his hand gripping the knife. He moved from room to room, hunting, but every turn took him back to where he began. The walls shifted, and the floors wavered, and he was bewildered. Each door led to a hallway that led to a dead end, the sharp arches of glass twinkling at him, promising pain. Exhausted and dizzy, he leaned into a corner, seeking an anchor, protection—though from what, he didn't know. He felt a loss of control. The house balked at his weight, at his entitlement to support. It closed in on him, deviating and rearranging itself until a hollow appeared, between walls, between floors, between worlds, and there the intruder was folded in, trapped, never to hurt again.

A house can be a prison, too.

When the woman woke, she sensed what had happened to her hunting husband. She picked up the knife. The house seemed different around her, heavier. She flung open the windows and kissed her son, who stilled within her embrace, transfixed by the bloodstained floor.

She carried him to the kitchen, where she cooked fluffy balls of akara, imbuing them with the new lightness in her heart, the aroma of frying beans shaking her son loose. They ate together, the deep freezer their table, and spoke of flimsy things, laughing and licking salty oil off their fingers, never once looking over their shoulders.

◊ ◊ ◊

ARIT'S UNCLE SHUTTERED THE WINDOWS of the paper building that night, then let the yellow pencil go. He pushed the cup of warm Milo to her side. What happens in a house stays in it, he told her, his fingers circling her left wrist—her drawing hand. What happens in the dark must never see the light. His voice had dropped the jokey register, cloaking her protests. His hairy hands traced further, drawing patterns on her skin she would never forget. Architecture is about negotiating borders, he whispered.

She was fourteen.

◊ ◊ ◊

THE WOMAN AND HER SON lived in peace in that house that was also a prison, in the certainty that they were safe and secure. The boy grew into a man. He married a short dash of a girl with shiny, dark skin and full, sagging cheeks. The new wife added her laughter to the house. Her songs rose like incense to the rafters.

When the woman lay dying, she pulled her son's wife close, and with breath that smelled of wilting vegetables, she whispered the story of the house that had protected her. The wife smiled at her mother-in-law's deathbed gibberish and patted her old, scarred hand and forgot.

She painted the house a baby pink, softening it, hoping for children to fill its spaces. She cultivated a garden. Her husband knelt beside her in the damp soil, and they planted tomatoes and aloe vera and lemongrass. She made him elaborate meals, and he wrote her elaborate letters. They made love in every room.

But the years introduced a sourness to their marriage. Her husband changed. He came home from his bank job frustrated—by customers who screamed and a woman supervisor who always demanded more and colleagues who didn't respect him—and he took these frustrations out on his wife.

The house stirred from slumber, moved in righteous anger—because hadn't it protected this man when he was only a scared boy? Waking to behold the rooms shuffled around her, the wife finally remembered her mother-in-law's story and knew her husband was gone. Her knees framed the new bulge in her stomach, and she cried with sadness and relief and indignation and gratitude.

◇ ◇ ◇

MADAM ONI SWITCHES ON the light in the master bedroom. "What you will find here," she says to the stock-still Arit, "is a big, fat nothing."

◇ ◇ ◇

THAT NIGHT, LATE, after her uncle had gone, Arit took an eraser in her dominant, left hand to the house they'd drawn together. Friction, friction, until the paper wore thin, until the shreds were indistinguishable from the rubber shavings, until her wrist ached where his fingers had circled first.

◇ ◇ ◇

THE WIFE WAS PREGNANT and alone, and she wailed and wept. The house watched, absorbing her tears, moisture beading on its walls, refracting the morning light.

The wife left the house with the taps running and the drains stopped, but she returned to dry floors. She threw rocks at the windows, but the cracks thinned and vanished before she could turn away.

"I didn't ask for your help," she screamed at the ceiling. But when a bowl of blended tatase peppers slipped from her hands and crashed to the floor in bloodlike splatters, she fell to her knees with a towel and wiped and wiped and wiped.

◇ ◇ ◇

THE FOLLOWING DAY, Arit's parents sat her down in their cluttered living room, her feet almost touching theirs on the threadbare rug. Outside, it rained. She wouldn't look up, afraid of what they would see in her eyes.

"Your uncle is dead," they told her, then broke down weeping. "We know this is hard for you—your favorite uncle." And they reached for her and embraced her, mistaking their own tears for hers.

"How?" Arit asked.

His house, her parents explained, it had just folded, collapsed. Late in the night. He was inside.

◇ ◇ ◇

THE WIFE LIVED IN the house her mother-in-law had built. Mother and child, healthy and happy. She seemed to forgive the house its action, and the house slipped into hibernation, content with this truce. The wife focused on her son, who grew tall and lithe. She kissed his forehead, broad like his father's, and pinched his cheeks, full to drooping like hers.

Years passed. The boy loved his mother. On his way home from school, he brought her gifts of plantain chips and kuli-kuli. He joined her in the kitchen, slicing yams and whisking eggs. When her lower back ached, he trod lightly on her, to massage the knots from her muscles, both of them sure that he would know when to step off, that he would mind the line between pressure and pain. She smiled at him, adjusting her depth of field so that he was her center, her star, and the house and what it held dissolved into a background blur.

◊ ◊ ◊

ARIT'S UNCLE HAD TAUGHT HER that architecture is the material realization of a vision. Why wouldn't it work the other way? Why couldn't a building's collapse also be a material realization of a want?

◊ ◊ ◊

SO, ONE AFTERNOON, as the wife walked past the closed door of her son's room and his too-young girlfriend said, "I'm not ready, stop, I'm not ready," she quickened her pace, pretending not to hear. But a house can't make such a choice. The boy was gone in the morning.

The wife took a hammer to a wall, wailing again, "Give him back," making no dent. Because he was just a boy, her boy, and she'd expected he'd have time to learn, to unlearn.

◊ ◊ ◊

ARIT NO LONGER DRAWS houses with her left hand. Instead, she uses her right. And she hopes that if she respects the power in a line, and is deliberate with it, and careful, she can atone.

Always logical, Arit.

◊ ◊ ◊

THE WOMAN REMAINED IN the house, seeking hints of her son in the skirting, in the junctions between walls and ceilings, in the dust patterns on windowsills, in the shaped shadows on floors.

The house gave her nothing.

And she responded in kind: she stopped painting; she stopped all maintenance.

Still, the house stood strong, stubborn in its principles, in the duty breathed into its foundations so many years before by the woman who needed it, and refused to crumble around the woman who resented it.

There is no gray zone with a house, it is all definite lines. How else could it stand?

◊ ◊ ◊

WHAT IS A HOUSE?

◊ ◊ ◊

AS MADAM ONI FINISHES the story of the house, Arit looks out to see the sun coming up. The rain has stopped.

"I woke one morning, and I was tired of searching for my son," Madam Oni says, breaking the silence. "Every angle in every room, every window placement, is a reaction to my son, to my husband, to my father-in-law. I'm living in that reaction, haunted by it. And I need this house to be fixed, so I can forget."

"There is no fixing," Arit says. An itch blooms angrily on her wrist, and she scratches. Friction, friction. "It doesn't work. No fixing, no forgetting."

Madam Oni shakes her head, rejecting Arit's conclusion. She presses her hand over Arit's, stopping it. "I can't believe that. I have to try. *We* have to try. Please."

Downstairs, a sustained sound, like the ringing of a tin cup, a cry in its hollow.

What does justice cost? What are clean hands left to carry?

Arit disentangles herself from Madam Oni and walks to the narrow windows. The new morning colors bleed into being. There is no fixing. A collapsed house cannot un-collapse. Rubble is also an objective expression of history. But Arit won't be its warden. She won't be stuck.

Soon, Arit will walk out of this house and never return. She will pick up a pencil with her left hand and sketch something light, something abstract. She is tired of paying, of carrying.

◊ ◊ ◊

A HOUSE IS A POT, a house is a bag, a house is a prison, a house is a supplication, a house is a justification, a house is a child on your back, weighing you down. A house is a house, and you can erase it, wreck it, tear it to the ground. A house is a house, and no, you can never forget, but you can walk away.

IMAGINE ME CARRYING YOU

THE ACCIDENT HAPPENED DURING THE HOLIDAY between my third and final years at university. I had escaped the house I lived in with my mother for Olivia's family mansion; turned off my phone for the weekend so my mother wouldn't call to ask what I was doing, who I was doing it with, and why I was doing it and ruining her reputation. When I turned it on around noon that Monday, my father's message was waiting after the too-bright, too-long booting of the device.

I called him as I drove home, tugging the smelly T-shirt from Saturday over the dress from Sunday night that showed too much cleavage. I hoped enough time had passed for the whiskey smell to become a vague suspicion rather than an indictment.

"The divorce has been final for almost two years, how am I still her emergency contact?" my father asked me, talking about himself first, as usual. "She needs to make you her next of kin."

And when I didn't respond to this, honking at an okada that got too close to my car, he added, "Where have you been? Ehn? During that crazy rain on Friday night, she hit someone on Ibadan Expressway. The poor girl didn't make it, unfortunately. But the family isn't calling police. There were many accidents that night, apparently. Your mother took it hard. She sent some money to the girl's family, for the burial and things. I think she's fine now sha . . . Are you driving? You should not be on the phone while driving!"

I got home to find my mother not fine. She was wrapped in her adire boubou, large and patterned with amorphous swirls of indigo, her face swollen with tears, fingers scratching at the arm of the leather sofa she was folded in. She was mewling—low and sad and heart-wrenching.

"Mummy," I said. I let my bag fall and moved to squat in front of her. "Daddy told me. I'm so sorry."

She said nothing to me. She rocked herself back and forth and made sounds that reminded me of a horror movie where the woman is haunted by her dead children.

Thinking that she might have spent the night in a police station, if we lived in a different country, I said, "We have to be grateful for the ineptitude of our justice system this one time." I was hoping for a stern *too soon* shake of the head, an exasperated eye roll, best-case scenario: an easing of her forehead creases. But my mother stopped rocking. She glared at me, eyes so wide and angry. Then she reached out to slap me across the cheek.

My tailbone hit the floor when I pulled back, shocked, *what the fuck* confused. She had never hit me before.

◊ ◊ ◊

THE GIRL'S FAMILY did not want my mother at the burial, but she wanted to go anyway. She made me call the deceased's brother over and over and over in her presence to ask for details. When the man realized my connection to his sister's death, he ended the call. The phone rang and rang after that, playing a ringback tune too melodious for the occasion.

"He's not picking up my calls," I said to her.

She raised her head from where it was buried in the crook of her arm on the dining table, her disheveled weave dipping into the bowl of yam pottage I had been urging her to eat.

"Can't you get anything right?" she spat at me, then lowered her head.

◊ ◊ ◊

"I HAD TO CARRY HER," my mother said, "after I hit her, and it was still raining, hard, like it was slapping my body, and I had to carry her, and she was heavy, like roughly your size, imagine me carrying you now, and there was blood everywhere, but she was making sounds, like, remember when you used to sleep-talk, and I was telling her don't die, don't die, don't die, and I put her in the back of the jeep, and I couldn't even see the road clearly on my way to St. Mary's, everywhere was flooded, but she died, she still died."

"Mummy," I began.

"I'm not asking you to say anything. I'm just telling you."

◊ ◊ ◊

MY MOTHER KEPT SOMETHING from the accident. I discovered it when she had fallen asleep on that sofa I had come to associate with her disintegration. It fell out of her limp hands to the carpet.

I picked it up and moved to a window to study it properly.

It was a temporary voter's registration card. Her name was Eyitayo Omolade Ogunlesi. She had a round face, round cheeks, round eyes, and a nose that looked like two circles joined together. She was twenty-four. Her blood group was O positive. She was from Osun State. She was five foot seven. She had registered at Obalende.

The card was curved at the corners. I ran my fingers around those corners, rubbing along the edge, waiting to be cut. But the edges were too blunt.

What was not on the card was who she was: lazy, smart, loved, student, smoker, nurse, self-aware, seamstress? Or if her mother, too, was refusing to wash herself, even two weeks later; if she had siblings, maybe a little sister who came home to realize the dress she had asked for and been denied was now free for the taking.

But I did not want to know.

I shoved the card into my back pocket.

◊ ◊ ◊

"I HOPE YOU'RE NOT going anywhere this weekend? Your parties can wait."

I hadn't been out since the accident. I resented this assumption that I would leave her in this state to go party with Olivia. Of course, I craved the foamy fuzziness that too many beers would bestow. Olivia thought I drank too much, which was silly because she drank more than me. But she opined that I was drinking away my mummy and daddy divorce issues, while she was drinking for fun, and that it made all the difference. But I wouldn't leave my mother like this. Why did she always expect the worst from me? It was the same way she cut my hair before my first day of secondary school because she was sure I would "become vain and, therefore, loose," the way she bought me packets of that fake slimming tea when I was off to university because she was sure I would gorge myself on "all that new freedom." She was always one step ahead, reprimanding me for a crime that had not been committed, correcting a mistake I had not yet even conceived.

"Or am I talking to myself?" she asked of my silence.

"Why?" Her request for me to stay home was strange.

"You're asking me why you shouldn't go partying? This is what I'm hearing?"

"Never mind," I mumbled.

She shook her head and walked away from me as if I were morphing into everything she feared.

◊ ◊ ◊

"WHERE'S THE CARD?" She threw open the door to my room, waking me from sleep.

"What?"

"I know you have the card. Give it back to me right now!"

My face was still in the pillow, but all dregs of sleep evaporated when she swept a hand over my desk, pushing things to the floor. I heard something break.

"Mummy, what the fuck?"

"Don't swear at me, you stupid child! Give it back now!"

Her boubou, the same one, slid all the way off her shoulder; one big brown nipple peeked out. I saw her collarbones, I saw her thin neck, I saw the veins strain against her skin when she screamed.

I jumped out of bed, reached for my jeans on the floor. I pulled the ID card out of the pocket and handed it to her. She yanked it out of my hand, her nails scratching me in the process.

Card held to chest, she took in a deep breath and walked away from me again.

◊ ◊ ◊

I CALLED MY FATHER in his new house with his new family. He had abandoned me with her. Left her, but left me too. Left me to be the sole recipient of her scrutiny and madness. But she should be his problem too. I didn't marry her. I didn't choose her. I didn't choose any of this. "Daddy, you need to come see Mummy. She is not fine."

"Oh, darling. I'm so busy but I'll see what I can do."

"I don't think she's well at all. And I don't know how to—"

"I said I'll see what I can do."

◊ ◊ ◊

MY FATHER SHOWED UP a week later with no notice. My mother was sitting in front of the TV, a rerun of *Family Matters*, with the volume turned down. I was painting my nails black at the dining table and smudged them when the jangle of the doorbell surprised me.

"Welcome, sir," I said to him.

He stood there for a moment as if remembering what it was like to come home to this family every night for twenty years—to a wife who insisted they go to important parties wearing matching ankara and a daughter who disappeared behind her bedroom door after the most minimal attempt at conversation. Then he smiled and pulled me into a hug, smearing my nail polish further.

"How is she?"

I shrugged within the hug, then stepped back to let him in.

"Mgbọ, Kemi, what's all this I'm hearing? What's going on?" He perched on the edge of the armchair adjacent to her beloved sofa.

I returned to my place at the dining table, pretending not to listen as I wiped off the ruined paint job.

My mother continued to stare at Steve Urkel pulling at his suspenders, not looking at her ex-husband, not responding.

"Kemi, da mi loun! I've never seen you like this; you're scaring your daughter."

She turned to him then, crying again. "Dotun. I killed another woman's daughter."

"Ah ah ah, maa sukun." He made to touch her, then retracted his hand. "Stop crying, it's not your fault."

"Whose fault is it?"

He was silent. Then, "The rain was bad that night and you told me yourself that the girl crossed the express? Everyone knows that's a recipe for disaster. Those overhead bridges aren't suggestions naa."

"But she died, Dotun."

My father sighed and rubbed his bald head. I noticed the glimmer of his new wedding band. I walked into the kitchen but stood at the door so I could still listen.

"You need to forgive yourself, Kemi. Forgive yourself and move on! Even the girl's family has forgiven you. The girl's own mother has forgiven you."

"That's only because the woman thinks she's being punished; that this is payback for some wrong she did."

"Well then, in that case, let it go. She's explained it away for you."

My mother went quiet for a long time. I started to move out of the kitchen, to call this intervention a failure, when she spoke again. "So," she said, "you're saying I'm the devil's messenger, abi?"

"What?" My father's response mirrored what my reflection was showing in the doors of the fridge: confusion.

"No, aren't you telling me that the devil used me to pay the woman back?"

"I said no such thing."

"You'd better go before the devil uses me to destroy you and that young girl you married!"

"She's thirty-four. Kemi, can't we talk like—"

"Dotun, please go! I don't know who called you here. It's that daughter of yours, isn't it? Leave me alone! Both of you! You, go home! Go! To! Your! Family!" She punctuated each syllable with a clap.

I heard the front door slam and then she was at the kitchen door, glaring at me. The tears she had been crying for three weeks were drying patchily on her unclean face; that boubou had begun to smell.

"You!" She pointed at me. "You better respect yourself."

◊ ◊ ◊

OLIVIA SENT A TEXT. *Where've you been? We're going to Escape tonight. Stella's sugar zaddy is paying. Lol. You down?*

Can't, I responded. *Mumsy isn't feeling well.*

◊ ◊ ◊

"WAKE UP." She was standing over my bed. I smelled her before I saw her.

"Ma?"

"I need you to take me somewhere. Please."

The addition of the *please* opened my eyes. I roused myself. "Where?"

She stood at the door of my room, watching me pull jeans on. I turned my back to her so she wouldn't see the unapproved tattoo under my left breast; it was too early for another lecture. I lifted my nightshirt and pulled on a tank top to replace it in an inelegant dance.

"I can't drive," she announced.

"Ma?"

"I tried to drive but I couldn't do it. The key wouldn't turn."

"Maybe if you give yourself some more time?" I faced her, safely covered.

She shook her head. "I'm selling it. Uncle Dele is coming to pick it up next week. He'll find a buyer."

"You're selling the jeep? But you love it."

"Of course I'm not keeping it," she said, as if I had proposed something foolish. "There's blood all over it."

◊ ◊ ◊

WE WERE QUIET IN the car except for when she would say "Left here," or "Slow down, don't let those LASTMA men stop us," or "Right after the roundabout." Being together this way felt a little like before the accident. We'd never had a smooth relationship, but there had been blips of goodness, notes of a normalcy I saw when my other friends interacted with their mothers. Like when we'd drive to the market together and she would sit so stiffly next to me, exaggeratedly, because she never trusted my driving and wouldn't relax until she was in the middle of a story from her wedding planning business. About a client's mother who acted like her daughter's wedding was all about her. Then she would assure me that she would never be that kind of narcissistic mother-of-the-bride, conspicuously segueing into asking me if I had a boyfriend. Or when we cooked together, or around each other, attuned to the other's movements, a choreography born of practice, of time, of intimacy: she, moving from the sink to put chicken in a pot, me leaving the cooker to wash a sieve or chopping board, never bumping. That is, until she criticized the way I stirred the afang soup or didn't close the tap all the way. Then *pop*, and we would be back to tense, closer to stalking boxers in a ring than dancers on a stage.

I recognized the sepia tones, narrow convoluted streets, and old colonial buildings of Yaba, but I didn't know where we were going. She asked me to park in front of a low gray fence and I swung the car between two buses. I squinted at the other vehicles, looking for clues. I found none. There were tall trees on the other side of the fence.

My mother looked straight ahead at the wall's chipped paint. There was no signage or poster to declare what was behind. I asked her no questions, just sat there, inhaling the three-week-long medley of her unwashed bodily scents.

A new bus sputtered to a stop behind us and a group of mourners stepped out. They wore different shades of black, different shapes of long faces. I looked away when someone glanced at us, curious; I looked away to find my mother's mouth open in a muted scream. I recoiled. I couldn't avoid her wide eyes, wide nose, wide mouth, as if she were being punched in the throat, her voice collapsed, her face doing all the wailing. I stared, transfixed, at this much emotion bleeding from my mother, until a car door slammed somewhere, shaking me.

After they disappeared behind the wall that I now understood enclosed a cemetery, I started the car. She did not stop me as I pulled out and drove. Her cries gained sound and followed us home.

◊ ◊ ◊

MY MOTHER'S BUSINESS MANAGER rang the bell and I opened to her worried face. I stepped out, not wanting anyone else to witness my mother's decline.

"She hasn't come in," the woman said to me. "It's over a month now and the clients are talking. Mrs. Okuboyejo wants her personally involved with her daughter's wedding. She's threatening to use another planner if she doesn't see"—she nodded behind me—"*her* at the next meeting."

We whispered in the foyer, as if my mother were our daughter who had been acting out at school, pulling other children's hair.

"I'll try my best," I said, turning to leave.

"There's something else." She cleared her throat, looked down at her jelly sandals. "She hasn't paid salary. I understand about the accident, but I don't know what to tell the other staff. They are complaining already."

"Can't you handle that?"

"Um, she took out most of the money from the company account. We're stretched thin. There's almost nothing left."

Almost nothing left? I nodded, pretending to be calm, pretending that I wasn't as worried as she was.

◊ ◊ ◊

"MUMMY, THE SCHOOL FEES portal is open. Daddy said to ask you for it."

She sighed long—that breathy hiss she'd been singing into every corner—and twisted away from me on the couch.

"Mummy?"

"I don't have it anymore."

I stood there staring at her crusty, pimply back above the neckline of the boubou. Patches of darker skin were appearing like maps to ghost towns.

"Did you give all my money to that girl's family?"

"Your money, is it?" She sat up. "Do you know Mrs. Bello called me? She said everyone sees you smoking weed at parties!"

What did one have to do with the other? I stepped back. Was this a distraction technique? But also, who snitched on me to a member of my mother's Gbagada Women's Association? That association whose judgment she used to measure everything I did. *What if someone from the association sees all your piercings? Please wear a camisole, I don't want people thinking I didn't give my only child home training.*

I wanted to ask her: Can you see yourself, mother, smell yourself—you whose favorite word is *reputation*? But if she was critiquing me, accusing me again, did it mean she was back to normal? Can we return to the part where you shout at me all of today and tomorrow, then leave me eggs in the frying pan as appeasement? Where we do our thing: you always exasperated, me exasperating you; you, frustrated by the way my adulthood limits your influence; me, freed by it. Distance of school making us think we like each other more than we do. Until I come home and do something newly stupid: like breathing, like smoking weed.

Even then, there was always a finiteness to our episodes, a grudging reconciliation, an admittance and acceptance of our faulty architecture. "She'll come around," I would tell Olivia when my mother went off about a hairstyle she thought was "too wild," or freeze me out for a week when I came home with bad grades. "This is her way, but soon she'll come around."

"Answer me," said my mother, who hadn't come around for weeks. "Smoking in public?"

"Mummy, what did you do with the money? Did you give it to them?"

"It's none of your business what I do with my money."

I thought: Can you be riled out of this everlasting grief? I said: "You know all of the money can't bring that girl back?"

But I calculated wrong again. Instead of lashing out and exhausting her agony/grief/guilt in one hopefully cathartic explosion, she deflated into the couch. She looked at me as if I were something vomited up.

"What's the point of paying all this money for your education if you're just going to shame me? You don't know there are people who want to be in your position." She sounded sad.

By my "position," did she mean alive? My chest went hot, like when I drank vodka straight. A clear picture of a round face with rounded features was imprinted behind my lids, taking up all the space. I knew then that the performance was never about me.

"Is your guilt enough to wipe away your own daughter's future?"

"No, you will not talk to me that way." She turned back to her couch, to her mourning.

I had terrible thoughts then. I thought: *You might as well follow her into the ground then, Mummy. Let's know you're serious.* I thought: *I hope that ID card can replace a living, breathing daughter o; shey you'll walk it down the aisle, teach it how to tie gele?* I thought: *Isn't it enough? Isn't five weeks enough?*

I thought: *Girl my mother killed, I hate you.*

◊ ◊ ◊

MY FATHER INSISTED THERE was nothing he could do about the fees. What he didn't add was that he had another family to care for now. I thought he was not outraged enough. I thought he was not angry enough because he had played his last card by leaving her to, in his words, "find myself," then promptly marrying again, and so would have to spend the rest of his life forgiving her for things that should not be forgiven. I said many things loudly to him over the phone, standing outside our gate so she wouldn't hear. My voice shook as I called him traitor, useless, wicked, disappointing.

"But sweetheart," my father said, "there's really nothing I can do. And you know better than to talk to me this way."

◊ ◊ ◊

"AT THE HOSPITAL, the woman . . . the girl's mother, she told me that there was one small girl working for her in her shop. She didn't know the girl was epileptic. Nobody told her. The girl did something bad one day, even the woman doesn't remember what, and she flogged that girl until she had a seizure. The girl died. That's why she doesn't blame me for the accident. She said she knew she would pay for that girl's death one day."

My mother offered this information in the hollowness of the kitchen. I stood at the sink descaling fish I had bought with my dwindling savings. My mother leaned against the door, watching and not helping with dinner. She smelled worse than the dead fish.

I said nothing, kept running the knife against the grain of scales.

"What does this mean for me? For you?" she asked. "What's the point of all my suffering to raise you right if you're dead?"

I scraped, and fish scales fluttered to my arms, my cheeks, my forehead.

"What if it just repeats, circles back? What if something happens to you because of me?"

I tilted my hands back and forth in the light and watched the fish scales change color. Then I plunged my hands back into the bowl of fish and screamed a lie. "Ouch!" Checking to see.

She rushed to me. "What? What? What happened? Are you okay?" Her rough palms all over my shoulders, my arms, my back. "What-what-what-happened-whaaat-is-it?"

I delayed, milked, measuring her reaction. Then I retrieved my whole hands. "Just a bone," I said, and her face cleared up too quickly, her relief puffing out in one stinking breath.

◊ ◊ ◊

POOL PARTY AT MAKI'S ON FRIDAY? *Some guys from Spice TV will be there, we have to represent!*

Then, five minutes later, *Is your mum OK now?*

Olivia's messages lay unanswered, a flash of the outside that made me feel even more claustrophobic in the house with my mother and her smells.

◊ ◊ ◊

MY FATHER TEXTED ME to say he was parked outside the house. I went out to him.

"Here, soup." He carefully handed over a huge bowl. It was still warm. Confused, I cracked open the lid to see lumps of meat and fish and ponmo swirling in the greens and yellows of egusi.

"She made it," he said, talking about his new wife whom I had refused to meet, though I had her face memorized from his profile photos: no makeup, huge ears. "Just a little something to take off some of your stress."

I didn't ask why she was making soup for us, why he was here bringing us her soup. I didn't ask if he'd changed his mind about my school fees, about my future. I nodded and hugged the bowl carefully to my chest.

"How is she?"

I shrugged.

"Sorry," he said, squeezing my shoulder. Then he got in his car and left.

◊ ◊ ◊

I MADE SEMO TO GO with the egusi and placed two plates for us on the center table.

"Mummy, food."

She looked away from the TV to take in the spread. Then she ate.

I sat beside her, tense, afraid that she would find me out, taste the other woman's sweat on her tongue, pour the palm-oil-heavy dish over my head.

Instead, she said, "Hmm, this is nice o."

And she smiled at me. I had forgotten her teeth this way. I had forgotten that the top left canine was higher, crowded out by the others. I had forgotten what it looked like for her cheeks to push up, crinkling her laugh lines, spreading her nose.

I smiled back, a morsel of semo frozen halfway to my lips, afraid to stain the moment.

Mummy, is that you?

◊ ◊ ◊

BOLSTERED BY THE PREVIOUS day's meal and how she touched my shoulder when I packed the plates to wash, I ignored that she had immediately disappeared into her room and stayed there. I was ready to understand this, her. Was she mourning the girl this hard so she could shift that fate away from me? But what would the point be if she was only erasing me with the loudness of this grief—a bigger production than she had ever made over one of my trespasses?

But things were changing now. A smile, a shower, then our worlds could be set straight. I could be a better daughter; stay home more, drink less, look beneath her tyranny for the good intentions. I would forgive her and defer my last year of school. We could work side by side for the year, planning her clients' weddings, our heads leaning close as we chose venues, decorations, colors. Is one dead girl equal to one year of your living daughter's life? I could live with that equation.

She was lying facedown in bed. The strong animal smell of my mother overwhelmed. I left the door open.

"I turned on the water heater so you can take your bath, Mummy."

I looked around the room. I didn't go in there a lot. It looked the same as it had when my father was around: dark because they never parted the blinds, the lumpy old duvet that I played games under as a child cast off to the side because of the heat, right down to an old pair of running shoes beside the bathroom door that he must not have thought worthy to take. Two years and those shoes still sat there waiting to cushion his feet.

"Mummy?"

"What?"

"I think a bath would make you feel better. You're getting bad acne."

"What would make me feel better is you leaving me alone. I have a headache." Her voice was muffled by the sheets.

I blinked. If a mother takes one step forward, how many steps back does it take to rebreak her daughter's heart?

The voter's card lay next to her. My hands itched to throw it into a fire.

I tried again, added a softness to my voice. "A bath might—"

She lifted her head. "I don't deserve a bath, okay? Leave me alone, please."

"Mummy."

"Just leave me, ṣ'ogbọ? Just go."

◇ ◇ ◇

FRUSTRATED BY THIS RETURN to stagnancy, I left her alone. If school was to be deferred, there would be a whole year where I'd be stuck with her anyway. With her madness and her moods and her odors. Would she ever overcome this? I needed to rage, to turn my brain to mush.

What's the weekend sayingggg? Let's party!

Olivia was quick with the details.

My mother had made me promise not to go out. She was scared that the fate of the dead girl was waiting for me in the shadows, on the roads, in strangers' faces and hands. But she had also promised to take care of me. Yet there I was, not being taken care of.

◇ ◇ ◇

THE COMBINATION OF LOUD MUSIC, mixed drinks, and too many of Olivia's "just try this one" pills meant that I returned home ill. My face was swollen and I had a fever. I couldn't remember enough of the long weekend to question if it had been worth it.

"Ugh, Mummy, you need to fucking shower. You stink," I said to the presence that appeared at my bedroom door, my pathetic state giving me immunity.

"What did you eat?" she asked, thinking my ailment was food poisoning.

I pushed my shoulders into a shrug. I groaned when she approached, cloaking me with her stench. I turned my face away when she squatted beside my bed.

The soft, wet cloth surprised me. She drew it over the back of my neck in a straight line. My body jerked in a shiver.

"Pẹlẹ," she said.

My mother who thought the solution to menstrual cramps was walking it off, and the cure to malaria was not to wallow. This same woman was now mopping my neck over a little fever. I was wary. But my focus shifted to the spot where the coolness of the cloth met the heat of my body, seeped into it, merged, and she, by extension, felt like a part of me.

I turned to face her. Her eyes were red red red.

"Mummy?"

Her mouth opened into an ugly cry, her yellowing teeth and white tongue adding another layer to the funk. She was sobbing but there were no tears. There were no tears. Were there no more tears for me?

"Mummy?"

"Don't die," she said at the end of a sharp exhalation. She closed her eyes. "Don't die."

"Mummy."

"I'm sorry," she said. "I'm sorry. Just don't die."

She kept stroking my neck but kept her lids shut, so stubbornly tight, really, really tight.

I couldn't see her eyes. She wouldn't open them, because she was not talking to me, was she?

"Don't die," my mother said to a dead girl, and I said, "Okay, Mummy." I laid my hands over hers and pressed her into my neck, holding on.

24, ALHAJI WILLIAMS STREET

ALHAJI WILLIAMS WAS A VERY LONG STREET. THE PLOTS were small, and many held clusters of flats. So we had enough time to see what was happening before it was our turn. My turn. By the afternoon the fever reached the fourth house, the rest of the street had braced for its arrival.

Ms. Williams owned the first house on the street named for her great-grandfather. They said that the Alhaji had rolled up his buba sleeves and mixed cement and sand along with the brick-layers, that he'd stood behind his architect and stabbed his finger at the blueprint, threatening to deafen with his orders: "No, the entrance should be on this side." "Add another arch here!" "I want that butterfly roof!" Ms. Williams was proud of this history, though maintaining the resulting gutter cost a lot.

Whenever I turned off Aderombi and onto our street, I stud-ied this house—repainted a bright white every Christmas to hide the dust, and topped with red clay shingles—trying to see the beauty in it. Maybe too many years had passed.

I was the only boy in my family, my mother's last child. Born on this street, bred on this street, I knew every metal gate, I knew the sore-throat horn of Mr. Joro's old Mercedes, I knew that if

I walked past the Obozos' at mealtime, their Rottweiler would push its jaws through the gap between wall and gate, barking until I was out of sight. I knew every daughter. I knew every son.

When we learned of Ade's death, my mother tut-tutted. "The poor poor widow," she said. "That poor poor woman." My mother was a widow too, but that day I understood the difference between a poor widow—my mother—and a poor *poor* widow: Ms. Williams. A poor poor widow is one who loses her son.

The street came together in mourning. My mother didn't believe children should grieve other children, so everything I heard, I heard from her. She turned amala as she narrated Ms. Williams's anguish. The woman had rolled and rolled on that fine Persian rug in her living room. My mother added water to the amala. The woman had torn at her silk kaftan, yanked at her curly weave, wept until her mascara left black blotches on the beige wool. That poor poor woman.

Ade was Ms. Williams's only child, so the pattern wasn't yet apparent when the fever crossed the street to number 2, Alhaji Williams, and took the Emenikes' youngest son. Everyone thought some bug was going around. Maybe it was the illegal refuse dump growing behind the bus stop, attracting dangerous flies. But when the third and fourth families—the Bellos and the Adeyanjus in number 3—both lost their youngest boys to the fever, people started whispering.

The Adeyanjus had three sons: Titus, John, and Bartho. Bartho returned from school one Friday with a high temperature and eyes that teared up when he coughed. It was over by night, his mother blinking at the cooling body in her arms. The Bellos lived above the Adeyanjus; and during that difficult period, Mrs. Bello brought over pepper soup and jollof rice so Mrs. Adeyanju wouldn't have to cook. A week later, when Mrs. Bello picked up the empty bowls, her youngest, Michael, was in bed because he, too, had a fever. The next morning, Mrs. Adeyanju sent pepper soup to Mrs. Bello.

◊ ◊ ◊

"ARE YOU OKAY?" my mother asked me each morning as I stepped out for JAMB class. I was taking the university entrance exams for the second time.

My older sister stayed with her boyfriend during the week because he lived closer to her office, and because she worried another girl would move in and take her place. "I'm not taking any chances," she would say to our mother, who didn't disagree.

On the weekends she came home, she'd sit at the dining table, tapping gingerly at her computer keys, careful not to unbalance the short leg held up with a flat stone. We often talked about getting a new table, or calling Lekan, the carpenter, but we never did. And during these visits, my mother would sit near the entry and prop open the wooden door to let in the breeze, while the screen kept out the mosquitoes. From a bowl in her lap, she'd string up beads of various sizes and colors on fishing line, between diamonds that could not be real, for her soon-to-be-married clients. I'd lie on the floor, working through practice questions, my belly flush with the cool terrazzo because we had no Persian rug.

Whenever my sister paused, raised her head, we would pause too, awaiting whatever she had to say.

"Do you think we should move?" she asked after the fourth boy died.

And my mother sighed, returning to her beadwork. "What's the point?" she replied.

It wasn't only her reluctance to leave this decrepit bungalow my father had died in, or her acknowledgment that we couldn't afford the rent anywhere else. When Mr. and Mrs. Anthony of number 5 knew it was their turn, they'd moved to Abuja with their five children. Their son had died anyway, just on a strange bed. There was no fleeing it.

My sister resumed typing, and I continued my math derivatives, my pen digging too deep into the paper, almost tearing it.

◊ ◊ ◊

THE MOTHERS ON THE STREET gathered some nights to mourn, to pre-mourn, to discuss the futility, but most of all, to share old fever remedies.

Mrs. Okocha sprinkled cayenne pepper on everything her son ate—fruits, garri, even ice cream, much to the boy's dismay. But when the fever came, he was dead before sunrise, unable to enjoy the taste of one last, cayenne-free meal.

Madam Rhoda rose every morning to grate baskets of ginger, which she steeped in hot water, then poured down her son's throat. When he passed, she held his head with her shredded fingertips.

Oga Tanko didn't have a wife, so he attended the meetings himself. He tried to freeze the fever away, installing a new air-conditioning unit at every corner. He curled up in bed with his son as the boy shivered. One morning, I saw heaps of broken ACs on the street outside his house, their white carcasses shining bright in the sun.

My mother proposed additional antidotes: boiled basil leaves and honey, vinegar in a lukewarm bath, lemongrass in hot water, raisin juice in hot water, mint, egg whites, turmeric . . . If she didn't have a suggestion before the meeting hour, she'd lean over my shoulder and ask me to ask Google.

BY THE TIME FLAT FOUR at number 11 lost their last son, nobody came together to weep, to light candles, to sing songs that were off-key but so beautiful, drifting down the street on the wind. Instead, they sent text messages—*We're sorry for your loss*—while watching their own sons, still breathing, waiting. Family silhouettes melded together in the windows, composite black monsters haunting my nighttime strolls.

I stood outside the JAMB center with my friend Junior, who lived at number 15. My father had attended the University of Ibadan, and though his reverent memories of that "great institution" did not reflect the fading campus Junior and I assessed from the backseat of his dad's car, we both filled it in as our first choice. It was Junior's second year of writing the exam, too. He hoped to study economics; I, engineering. But at the center's gate, considering a half-peeled poster announcing the test dates, Junior said, "What's the point?"

I agreed.

We went to a pharmacy and pooled money to buy a thermometer. "What's the normal body temperature?" Junior asked.

I asked Google. "Thirty-seven degrees Celsius."

He raised his T-shirt and stuck the thermometer in his armpit. As we waited, we watched the passing cars. He pulled it out, and we crowded over it, squinting.

"Thirty-seven point two?" he asked.

I leaned in. "Thirty-seven point one."

Then it was my turn.

He shook the thermometer, and when I told him to wipe the end on his shirt, we laughed.

I placed the device under my arm, hugging my elbow tightly. I sent a message: *Be cool, be cool.* And when I pulled it out, a whiff of sweat dissipating in the air between us, Junior read, "Thirty-six point nine." I looked away from the envy he tried to hide.

We shared a joint at the back of Iya Risi's buka, staring at the goats and cooped chickens that would soon be lunch. We argued over which of Brymo's albums was the best, if *Klĩtôrĩs* showed a dip in his arc, if he was maybe the Fela of our generation.

"If all your friends were in hell, would you still go to heaven?" Junior asked me.

I blew out smoke. "I don't know, man."

◊ ◊ ◊

JUNIOR AND I SAT opposite Ms. Williams's house, on the log of a tree some NEPA people had cut down without asking the street's permission. They said it had been disturbing the power lines. The street looked different without the branches bowing over the sidewalk, weighed down by the fruit we called "fruit." The day the tree was felled, I'd walked right past the corner before realizing it was ours.

"Have you seen Ozzy around?" I asked. My mother had asked me the same question before I'd left the house that morning. He lived at number 14 and was next.

"At all—why?" Junior coughed and I watched his face before

shrugging. He was friendlier with the other boys on the street, so would know what happened before me. I couldn't care less about them; football back in the day was fine, but now I felt awkward in their presence, in their conversations about FIFA or the girls in JAMB class who didn't wear bras. Junior was my only friend. He spoke about these things, too, but it felt different.

"I heard some guys yarning about going away," he said, "as if we didn't all hear together that oyinbo medicine couldn't save Chibuzo."

Chibuzo, the youngest son of the old couple at number 12, had been in America doing his MBA at Columbia. When the call from the New York hospital came at three on a Sunday morning, they were already by the phone, awake and waiting.

Junior wiped his brow, and I reached over to grab his wrist to twist his watch toward me. My real purpose was to check his temperature. His skin was warm in my palm. But maybe it was just the midday sun.

"Ozzy's a big guy," he said.

The last time I'd seen Ozzy, he'd been lifting weights in Bolu's backyard, as always, and I couldn't tell if Junior meant that Ozzy would take care of himself, or that he'd die with new muscles, strained and flexed and defiant.

◊ ◊ ◊

HARMATTAN ARRIVED A MONTH after Chibuzo's passing, coating Alhaji Williams Street with layers of dust. The dust remained untouched this year, no *please wash me* scrawls on car windows, no children dragging sticks, few footprints.

Junior and I still left the street every morning, though not for the JAMB center. And every morning, I'd squint at his chapped lips, gauge the redness of his eyes.

The longest period between deaths had been three months— three months in which a fragile hope bloomed.

"Should I roll?" I asked.

Junior shook his head, but I shrugged it off. I understood.

"So, what do you want to do?"

He kept kicking his Air Force 1s in the dust without looking up.

"What's up, man?"

Then he leaned in and hugged me. I felt his wetness on my neck.

◊ ◊ ◊

MY MOTHER CAME TO LIE in bed with me. She smelled of Irish Spring and akara. "Se Bo'timo" played from my speakers.

"Baby," she whispered.

"Is he dead?"

I felt her nod in the dark.

I let out what began as a sigh and ended as something else. "He knew," I said around the scratchiness in my throat.

She leaned closer and stroked my head.

◊ ◊ ◊

AFTER JUNIOR'S DEATH, I'd stare at the same page of my practice book for hours on end, my eyes bloodshot and itchy from the dry winds of harmattan and the tears I wouldn't cry. There was nobody to nudge in laughter, nobody to tease about shoddily wrapped joints, no Junior to just walk beside—in silence, in solidarity. All these undoable and unsayable things weighed me down so that I felt like one of Fela's zombies.

Over her bowl of beads, my mother watched me. Then she went from door to door, trying to convince the people of Alhaji Williams Street to resume the vigils, to show up for the meetings.

"These losses are both personal and communal," I heard her telling Mr. Francis when he came to return her empty Tupperware. His wife had shaved her head and now wore only black. "We need to hold each other in these times. We need to come together. Now more than ever."

That night, the street came together under a full moon that blessed our tipped and mourning heads. My mother allowed me to accompany her. "You're no longer a child," she said, pressing her lips to my hairless chest.

We stood, we knelt, we sat, we leaned against cars, taking the grime onto our clothes. We held hands and sang. My mother raised a Yoruba song, a familiar tune she'd begun to hum around the house.

> *When you see the kob antelope on the way to the river—*
> *Leave your arrows in the quiver,*
> *And let the dead depart in peace.*

The men cried and the women wept and my mother leaned all of her weight against me.

◊ ◊ ◊

MY MOTHER MADE ME slice open the neck of a chicken and sprinkle the blood on our front door. I held its wings together, then placed my slippered foot on its head. The bird heaved and struggled under me as I sawed. When it stilled, my eyes misted.

This was the newest thing on the street: bloodstains on the gates and doors of the untouched houses. Maybe the fever would pass over, as it did the children of Israel.

I heard from Laolu, a boy at number 31, that it had been my unreligious mother's idea. As we bought eggs and sardines from the mallam, he recounted his mother's report that my mother had made a speech at one of the neighborhood meetings, quoting the Bible. My family went to church at Christmas and at Easter, but after my father's death, even those days were not certain.

I avoided the front door. The smell disturbed me, and it had started attracting flies. I went around the house and entered through the kitchen.

"No, you have to go through the door," my mother insisted. "You have to go through the door!"

But after Tolulope of number 17 succumbed, she poured a bucket of water and scrubbed the blood off.

◊ ◊ ◊

MY AUNT CAME TO VISIT, bringing huge bundles of unripe plantains. It felt like a goodbye. At number 21, the littlest Adejo boy was burning in his mother's arms.

My mother and aunt sat in the kitchen, picking beans. My aunt was older by ten years and very resourceful. She'd introduced my mother to my father, arranged my sister's first job, secured me a personal room in the general hospital—a feat—that year I broke my leg playing football.

I walked in and they fell silent, their fingers busy but their eyes on me as I moved from the sink to the cupboard, drinking water, taking a handful of groundnuts from the bowl. I left to wander the empty street, perhaps hoping that by escaping their stares I could escape their worries, too.

When I returned that night, my aunt summoned me to the living room. She was knitting some huge thing, stripes of different colors, my mother asleep beside her. "How old are you now?" she asked me.

"Seventeen," I said.

She eyed me, head to toe, then flicked her wrist for me to go.

◊ ◊ ◊

I HAD DREAMS OF HELLFIRE. I think it was hellfire. It burned the University of Ibadan, the one legacy I'd hoped to continue for my father. It burned my fantasies of ever seeing Brymo in concert, or of watching my sister finally marry her boyfriend. And sometimes, from the inferno, Junior would call out to me.

I'd wake up from these dreams, stick the thermometer in my armpit, and stare at the numbers—36.9, 37.2, 37.3, 36.9, 37.1—until they blurred into black smudges and I drifted back to unconsciousness.

For the JAMB exam, we were required to bring photocopies of our forms and receipts. I piled all my documents in the backyard and set them aflame.

◊ ◊ ◊

MRS. FAFUNWA OF FLAT TWO at number 22 had only daughters. She wasn't alone in this situation, but she was the most vocally grateful about it.

She would go to the pharmacy and announce her need for Nixoderm, teasing the girls for their touches of eczema, reveling in the other parents' envy. After Sunday lunch, the four of them took long strolls along the street, talking about the future: when the first one would get married, when the second would give her grandchildren, when the third would buy her a new car. The girls would giggle, hug, lay their heads momentarily on their mother's breasts.

When they encountered their neighbors, subdued from a recent or imminent loss, Mrs. Fafunwa would respond brightly, asking if all was well at home, tucking a braid behind a daughter's ear, smoothening the blouse of another.

She never went to the meetings, but stood on her veranda, humming gaily while watering two tall potted plants, to ensure she was noticed. She bought a sticker for her Toyota Camry that read DAUGHTERS ARE THE FUTURE!

One Monday, she returned from her beauty salon to find her daughters dead in their beds, knives in their chests.

Mrs. Fafunwa screamed into the night. Nobody came to her, nobody cried with her. If the street knew who did it, no one would say. When she put the final box in her car and left Alhaji Williams Street for good, not a single neighbor waved goodbye.

◊ ◊ ◊

"THIS STREET IS CHANGING O, sister. Hmmn. It's changing."

Beneath my mother's words, my aunt's knitting needles clicked a rhythm, the colorful thing growing but not yet acquiring a shape I could decipher. I sat at the dining table, reading a news report about a woman in Ipaja who'd birthed a yam. The accompanying photo showed her cradling the tuber in her arms, her head resting against the bedpost, eyes closed.

My mother was horrified by what had befallen Mrs. Fafunwa's daughters, frustrated at the street's silence.

"Leave it, aburo," my aunt said now. "*Fi lẹ*."

With the needles paused, I looked up to find my aunt watching me. Under the weight of that gaze, I turned back to the photo of the new mother.

Click click, the needles resumed.

◇ ◇ ◇

THE FOLLOWING FRIDAY, my mother sat on the balcony, beading in what little breeze the night might give, while my sister was in her usual spot at the table, pecking at her laptop. I lay on the sofa, staring at the armchair that had been my father's favorite. "Just like your father," my mother would say about my stillness. "Sometimes I wouldn't remember he was around. Doing like a ghost, that man."

The lights went out and my sister hissed, cursing NEPA. My mother's bowl clattered to the floor.

"Is there fuel for the generator?" My sister was speaking.

I just stared into the darkness. If the lights came back and I was not on the sofa, would it be easier for them?

"Did you hear me? Boy, are you listening?"

I could hear her, but I wasn't listening. I was on a cliff, terrified to look down lest the blackness reach up to swallow me whole.

◊ ◊ ◊

I WOKE THE NEXT MORNING to discover my sister at the foot of my bed, peering over me as if trying to memorize me, scaring me fully alert. She told me to get dressed, that she was taking us to the new amusement park on the expressway. We were having a family day.

My mother had fried chicken wings for the journey, and we hummed along to a station playing songs from the decade before: Tony Tetuila, Eedris Abdulkareem, Daddy Showkey, the works. My mother wore a borrowed cap that looked too young for her wrinkled face. From the backseat, I watched them, imagining that I wasn't there, that the fever had already taken me, that they were alone together, on a long drive, singing and breathing one another's exhalations.

Then 2Face's "Enter the Place" interrupted my premonition, compelling me to return.

At the park, I sat alone on the Twisting Wheel while my mother waved from below with shaking hands. The whole outing seemed an act of preparation, a test of our readiness. A couple above me was squealing and laughing. My sister swung an arm around our mother's shoulder, drawing her closer. I shut my eyes as we began to move. We went higher and faster. My heart expanded, the sensation like a chicken struggling to break free of my chest.

My salty tears burned my dry, cracked skin.

◇ ◇ ◇

AFTER IBRAHIM OF NUMBER 23 DIED, my sister moved
back home. She drove her boyfriend's car, commuting hours to
work and back in traffic. I quit even pretending to study for the
JAMB exam, and instead spent my days listening to all of Brymo's songs and changing the order of my favorites, between "Fe
Mi," "Alajo Somolu," "1 Pound," and "Prick No Get Shoulder"
(which I lowered whenever my mother entered my room). My
mother attended to her beadwork. Coral beads, glitter beads;
overlapping lines, interwoven lines. She showed us photos of
her brides, happy women grinning in traditional ceremonies,
powdered necks exhibiting her creations. When night came, we
stayed up late, the three of us, watching Africa Magic.

On one of these nights, I emerged from my room to find that
my aunt had returned. She stood by the front door, whispering
with my mother and sister.

They turned to me, these women who were my family. "We
need to talk to you," they said.

There was a way to escape the fever. My aunt knew a man who
could take me away. I would be alive, but somewhere else. A different realm. Inaccessible to them, but alive. Alive, alive. Another
boy on the street had escaped like this, but the man would not say
who. A family on Alhaji Williams Street had buried a wrapped
bundle of cloth instead of a son.

My mother pressed her ashy harmattan lips into a straight
line, and I could tell she felt betrayed—by her neighbors, by the
street. Still, she was willing to keep a secret, too. A betrayal for
a betrayal.

I lay on my bed, staring up at the fan, deliberating what to take with me, uncertain if I could take anything at all. Round and round and round.

My mother knocked on my door and came in. "Whatever happens," she said, then stopped talking.

"What's the difference?" I asked.

"What, baby?"

"If I die, or if I go away. What's the difference?"

She pushed until I made space for her to lie beside me.

"You'll be alive," she said. "It'll be different for you."

I remained quiet. I couldn't hope, but I could let her.

◊ ◊ ◊

"MAYBE OZZY WAS THE OTHER ONE," I suggested, "the other boy who disappeared." After the funeral, his family had left the street to visit his uncle and never returned. A padlock hung from the rusting gate of the abandoned house.

"It's possible. That mother of his was very, very secretive. You know, she never told me where she bought her snails. Ordinary snails, as if telling me would make them less delicious for her. She kept postponing." My mother gripped my sweaty palm. "Maybe she was the smart one here."

My aunt came to tell us it was time to go. I changed my T-shirt, then changed it back. I picked up Brymo's *Tabula Rasa*, an album Junior had given me, then returned it to my desk. My aunt handed me the sweater she'd been knitting; it smelled of her oud perfume. "In case it's cold," she said.

I hugged my mother, then my sister, then my mother again. My sister whimpered, but my mother remained stoic. She would wait till morning, then give over to her grief, and the neighbors would know that she, too, had lost her son.

When you see the kob antelope on the way to the river—
Leave your arrows in the quiver,
And let the dead depart in peace.

I lay in my aunt's boot, on a blanket to cushion the ride. A blanket and a bottle of water. My sister whispered a heartsick goodbye. My mother knelt in the gravel that must have been digging into the skin of her knees. She took my hands to her lips. Her eyes were squeezed shut, denying me access—perhaps protecting me from what I would see. She released me only when my aunt lowered the lid. I felt the shutting click in my chest; it was a flattening. The darkness pressed down. I opened my mouth to let the air out.

THINGS BOYS DO

CHILDREN CAN BE CRUEL, YOU KNOW?

THE FIRST MAN STANDS at the bedside of his sweating wife. He is watching their baby emerge from inside her. What he does not know is that he is watching their son destroy her insides, shredding, making sure there will be no others to follow. This man's wife is screaming and screaming, and the sound gives the man a headache, electric like lightning, striking the middle of his forehead. He reaches out to hold her hand, to remind her of his presence. But he is surprised by the power of her latch, this strength born of pain, the way she crushes the bones of his fingers. He has to bite down to prevent himself from crying out.

And here is the baby, bloody and outside for the first time. The first man flinches at the sudden appearance of white eyeballs in the midst of the slimy red of birth.

"Um," the doctor says, frowning. "You have a son."

The first man leans down to catch the mumbled words from his wife's mouth. "Yes, hon. He's alive," he reassures her. The whites of the baby's eyes are imprinted in his mind, behind the headache, like an image from the past, blurred and clouded by time. He looks up to the doctor, who is still holding onto the baby, brows furrowed. "He's alive, right, doctor? Is everything fine? Isn't he supposed to cry?"

The doctor looks everywhere but at the first man. They fuss around, the doctor and the nurses, snipping, cleaning, moving.

"Doctor?" the man prompts.

"Mr. Man, you have a son! Congratulations! A living, breathing boy!"

◊ ◊ ◊

THE SECOND MAN HUFFS beneath the weight of his wife. The Ikeja General Hospital has sent them home even though his wife is still bleeding from the birth. "Sorry, no space," the head nurse told him, her attention moving so easily to the next patient. "Take her home; everybody bleeds."

The second man's mother holds open the door to their apartment, cradling the baby like an expert. She trails them to the bedroom, where the man gently lowers his wife to their bed— still messy with signs of frantic packing for the hospital. Once his arms are free, the mother transfers the baby to him, as if she has been waiting to rid herself of the infant.

"Maami," he starts to say, but his mother leaves the room.

The baby is sleeping and his eyeballs move around beneath his thin lids. The second man is repulsed by this movement, this unconscious shifting, like a buried thing digging its way up. The man is then discomfited by this reaction to his child. He deposits his new son in the cradle that smells like wood polish, then goes to find his mother in the kitchen.

"Maami, will you make black soup for her? Will that help?"

The mother is staring out the kitchen window, her fingers steeping in a bowl of uncleaned tilapia. "That baby is not yours, I'm sure of it."

"Maami, please. Don't start this rubbish again."

"That baby is not yours; I can swear on it! I know it. I feel it." Her hands move again, lifting a gill flap, gutting the fish with a soft snap.

◊ ◊ ◊

THE THIRD MAN WALKS into the dining room to find his wife dozing off while their baby quietly suckles at the feeding bottle's nib. The image he encounters is this: her neck tilted backward and to the side so that the muscles seem contorted unnaturally, the tendons and veins pushing against skin. For a moment, he is sure she is dead.

She jerks awake when he tries to lift their son from her arms. Her hands instinctively tighten, then loosen. "Thanks," she whispers, her eyes drifting to close again. The man is impressed at how quickly she seems to have bonded with the baby they accepted from the arms of a teenage mother—whose name they were not allowed to know—only three weeks ago.

The third man rocks the baby the way they were taught at adoption classes. Softly, softly, back and forth. The baby's eyes flutter open and the man smiles down at his son, his first child, his baby. "Who's a good boy?" he sings, hoping that a bond will grow between them too. "Who? Who?"

The baby does not smile, but do babies this young even smile? The third man now feels silly because of what seems like a stern

look from the infant, as if the voice he has put on is simply ridic-
ulous, beneath him. How does one feel embarrassed in the sight
of a three-week-old baby? He frowns at his child, noticing for the
first time some flecks of gray in his irises. He blinks, startled, but
the gray is gone. A wink, a flash, a warning.

"You're not a good boy," the man whispers, queasy, no longer
singing, no longer rocking. "Are you?"

◊ ◊ ◊

THERE WAS ANOTHER BOY, ONCE. But that was so long ago.

◊ ◊ ◊

THE FIRST MAN IS ALONE with his son, again. His wife is in
the hospital, again. Since the birth, six months ago, hospital
visits and extended stays have become commonplace in their
household. Money is running out. The first man worries about
money; he worries about his job—all the time off he's been asking for; he worries about his wife; he worries about their baby.

But that's not true. He doesn't worry about the baby. The
baby is fed and cared for by his extended family network in Abeo-
kuta. His cousins and friends take turns helping out. What the
first man is really worried about is himself.

The first man worries for himself when he is alone with
Jon. Jon is what his wife insisted on calling their son. Short for
Jonathan—that man in the Bible only known for being a very
good friend to David. This fear of his son, for himself, it is a body
thing; a visceral thing; a flinching, recoiling, chilling thing. What

father is frightened of his own child, scared to hold him, scared to be looked at by him, to be really seen by him?

◊ ◊ ◊

THE SECOND MAN'S WIFE is dead, and now he is alone with Johnny, their six-month-old son. The barrage of love and support that immediately followed his wife's demise has slowed to a trickle. The bowls of rice and soup have stopped coming. His brother has gone back to Abuja. His cousin no longer stops by on the way to drop her kids off at school. The second man is alone. With Johnny.

His mother showed up at the burial, her nose in the air. But she did not make a scene. She did not hold Johnny, no, but she did not bring up more preposterous accusations about his wife's fidelity either, about the strange face of his son that she insists does not belong in her family lineage.

The second man watches Johnny roll from his back to his stomach on the multicolored mat splattered with ABCs; then to his back; then to his stomach. Back and forth. Back and forth. Back and forth.

The man backs away to the other end of the room, one foot behind the other. He sits in the armchair that still holds the cloying scent of his wife's shea butter. Back and forth, his baby turns, fists flailing, chubby legs kicking. The second man closes his eyes against this familiar feeling. The sight of his pivoting son makes him dizzy, askew, off-center.

◊ ◊ ◊

THE EMAIL WAS SHORT: *I can't do this anymore. Adopting this baby changed me. I need to find myself again. And if I do, I'm not sure I'll want to return. Be kind to J-Boy. Be kind to yourself.*

The third man reads the email every morning before getting out of bed. He reads it again this morning. Then he checks for new messages.

"Fuck," he whispers when he reads the newest text. The latest nanny has quit. *I'm sorry, but I have to go back to the village to care for my family.* Bullshit, the man knows, it's all bullshit. The ninth nanny in the three months since his wife's been gone. The excuses are always unbelievable, unimaginative.

The third man leans over the cradle beside his bed. J-Boy is awake. Does the boy ever sleep? "Why are you sending everyone away, J-Boy? Why?"

Because the common denominator is the boy, isn't it? The wife leaving, the nannies scurrying out the door, unable to articulate what they are balking at. Overcome, the third man slams his open palm against the side of the cradle. "Why? Why? Why?"

His hand is throbbing now, with pain, with shame, but the baby does not react, does not flinch. He is just staring, still staring, as if he has expected this all along: this breakdown, this debacle, this undoing. Looking at his heaving father like, *well*, like, *hello*, like, *I knew this* you *would show up soon.*

◊ ◊ ◊

THAT BOY FROM SO LONG AGO. He was just another boy. The same way our three men once were just three boys. Just three boys doing things boys do.

◇ ◇ ◇

THE FIRST MAN CAN no longer sleep at night. Not while it is just him and Jon alone at home. His wife has gone to live with a cousin in Seychelles; she needed bed rest and ocean breeze after the trauma of the birth. When he opened his mouth to protest what seemed to him like abandonment, she had looked at him so sadly, disappointed, shutting him up.

These days, he catches an hour or two of sleep when he can convince someone to come over, leaving his dwindling friends disgruntled because they thought they were coming to hang out with him, not feed his baby while he naps on the couch, drool glistening on his beard. "I'm not your fucking babysitter," his friend Joy said, plopping the baby on his chest, jolting him fully awake.

The first man's nights are fraught with a fear of Jon that rises from the top of his stomach, acidic and pungent, like the beginning of a burp. Tonight, he moves slowly toward the cradle, as if afraid of what he will find. But there, Jon is awake, staring at the turning fan. The baby becomes aware of his presence, and his eyes move in an arc from the ceiling fan to his father's face. His face reddens; his mouth trembles; he begins to wail.

The first man's fatherly instincts kick in. He tamps down his fear. He picks up the baby, pats his back. The wailing stops, but only because the baby's mouth has now affixed to his exposed shoulder. There is a sharp sting that sends the man's eyes backward, upward. How many teeth does this eight-month-old baby have? How can they be sharp enough to cause such precise, penetrating pain? He gets a finger between and pulls the child off with a smacking sound.

He resists the urge to fling Jon back into the cradle; jaws clenched, he lowers his still son. There is no more wailing.

This is his life now: downgraded to managing social media for a small brand that pays peanuts, but allows him to work remotely. This is his life: nappies that stink, formula that smells sickly sweet, and a baby that bites him too often.

He distractedly rubs against an old bite mark adorning his wrist. Then he wipes saliva off his shoulder, wincing at the rawness. Sitting in front of his laptop, he clicks to the Troubled Naija Fathers Forum he's found recently. *I think my baby hates me*, he types. The keyboard clacks echo around him. *He has taken everything from me. I am afraid of my baby. Is this normal?* Before he submits the entry, he remembers to make himself anonymous. Then the first man leans back into the chair, glancing briefly at his now-gurgling son. Is that a gurgle or a laugh? He turns back to his screen. The first man waits.

THE SECOND MAN FEELS seen when he reads the post on the popular forum. *Yes!* he wants to scream at his phone. What he does instead is move to another room, one where Johnny isn't present. He hunches over the device, afraid that his son—not even a year old—will somehow prevent him from replying to this post.

> YESSS!!! I feel the exact same way! I want to be a good father, but it feels impossible with this child. I hate to say it, but I feel like his appearance in my life has ruined me. My wife is dead, my mother won't talk to me. My friends avoid

me now. I am afraid to be alone with my own child . . . His very existence has undone me! Is this a medical problem? Something about a version of myself existing outside of me disrupting my balance? And is there a solution? Do I need therapy??? Sorry to ramble, but I feel so strongly about this!!! HELP US!

Then the second man hits send. He does not make himself anonymous.

◊ ◊ ◊

THE THIRD MAN, who has been eyeing the same post in the forum, clicks on the new and only comment.

He recognizes the name of the commenter immediately. His fingers spring off the mouse and hover over it, as if electrocuted.

There is no such thing as coincidence.

No, no, no, the third man thinks. He has not allowed himself to think about this person, about what he represents, in so long.

◊ ◊ ◊

YES, CHILDREN CAN BE CRUEL, evil even.

So long ago, when three boys cornered their classmate, the new boy, the slight boy with asthma who wheezed at the back of biology class, the boy begged to be left alone.

"Please, let me go," he cried. He promised his pocket money, the chocolate bars, to slide all his dinners to them, to iron their uniforms, to make their beds, to do their chores, to tend their portions of the school garden, to fetch their water, to do all their assignments. He promised everything. "Just don't put me in there," he begged. "Please, that space is too tiny," he cried. "Please. Please."

But boys will be boys, right? The three best friends bundled him up and stuffed him in the locker at the back of the abandoned woodwork shop. He scraped at the wrists of their gray uniforms; his head wagged back and forth, left and right; he pleaded with his eyes, with the veins bulging in them, with his wails; he clawed at their faces, bit at their shoulders, thumped at their chests, scratched at their foreheads. But he was nothing but a whiff of a boy. They snapped the padlock shut, giggling, smacking each other on the back, in mirth, in solidarity.

How easily attentions shift. What should have been half a class period became one, two, three. How easily boys can be distracted by other social activities, other friends, other weak students to tease. How easy it is to forget.

◊ ◊ ◊

AFTER THEY HAVE CONFIRMED what their bodies already know as true—through furtive private messages: *Is that you? The same one? From Ibadan High School?*—the first man, second man, and third man wait till the dead of night. They wait till they think they cannot be seen, when Jon, Johnny, and J-Boy are asleep; and then, with trembling fingers, they search the event they are all thinking about. The event. The Event of their boyhoods.

Over a decade later, the search results are not many, and he is faceless, but there it is: *Adebayo John—Gone Too Soon. Discovered by his three friends, killed by an asthma attack.* Not looking at each other, they lied to teachers, to their parents, then to themselves, revising. Each boy leaving the school, one after the other, to begin their forgetting. Of Adebayo John, who never did anything to them.

Watch as these men, who were once boys, look to their sleeping sons, now alert to the possibilities. The terror latches onto wrists, yanks them in. They look to their sons who have taken everything from them, who are still taking everything from them. The sons bound to them forever.

And two weeks or three months or four years from now, when these men try to rid themselves of their sons: abandon them with relatives or on a park bench wet from rain, they will never be able to walk away. Because they can never be sure where a haunting ends and paranoia begins.

But right now, watch them behold their sons—terrified by the possibilities—with hitched breaths, ticking pulses, raised hairs. And do you know, terror can feel like being trapped in a dark, tiny place, with no space to move? Like a locker, like a coffin.

BIRDWOMAN

FELICITY WAS BORN UNHAPPY. SHE WAS CONCEIVED when her parents were young and unmarried. They wedded immediately after the pregnancy was confirmed, then proceeded to use religion to punish themselves for as long as Felicity lived with them. There were evening prayers filled with loud supplications to God for forgiveness while she knelt there feeling every inch the mistake that they perceived her to be. There was the remittance of 50 percent of their income to the church, so that she never got those new shoes or money to go on the class excursion to Olumo Rock.

She grew up unhappy, too, sharing a tiny room with an older cousin who took the frustrations of being unemployed in a thriving city out on Felicity—slaps and kicks that left marks long after the physical scars had healed. Even when she ran away from home at nineteen—her bag heavy with money she'd stolen from her family—she remained unhappy. She paid for an apprenticeship at a tailor's shop on the other side of Lagos, where she excelled. When she became assistant manager after a few years, she promptly poached all her employer's good tailors to start her own business. But even then, though she was surrounded by the well-oiled machinery of her successful business, happiness eluded her.

Today, Felicity is a tall woman of forty-five with big feet and round shoulders that hunch forward. Her mouth is downturned and her thin bottom lip juts out, giving her a permanent look of one who has eaten raw bitter-leaf. She is still unhappy and her tailors sometimes attribute her constant displeasure to her unmarried status.

"If man for dey, shebi im go dey smile?" they whisper among themselves. But men do nothing for Felicity and she looks on, oblivious to meaning, face as blank as calico cloth, when one stares at her too long.

Felicity is on her way to buy sewing thread in bulk from Agege Market. She likes to do the shopping herself as she trusts no one. Her footsteps are heavy on the market streets cluttered with Gala wrappers and unlucky lottery tickets stained pink by the juice from baskets of tomatoes. Her right arm hugs her handbag tight to herself while her left hand further protects it from probable grasping hands. She has been robbed before; her stern sneer hadn't prevented pickpockets from approaching.

She walks past the men stretching out pairs of jeans—snapping the fabric taut to show its tensile strength, calling out to women younger and prettier than she is. She walks past the shops where the girls selling bedazzled aso-oke and lace cloth look right through her, searching for potential customers. But when she meets a crowd in her path, Felicity stops.

It is her birthday today but she has told no one. There is no one to tell. She has no friends and she is not sociable enough with her staff to have them pretend to care. On this day every year, Felicity does something out of character. One year, she made herself a long red dress from see-through chiffon. She stood in front of her mirror for hours in this dress, turning this way and that—never smiling, just staring. As she studied herself, she mentally tucked in a flab here and trimmed a bulge there, but she wasn't satisfied. She peered into the mirror, her mind hacking away at her person—too grounded, too heavy—imagining she was nothing but bones and that the red dress fluttered in the air.

Another year, she bought herself a huge bowl of ice cream from the Big Treat Supermarket down the street and gave her staff the day off. Amongst the immobile sewing machines and headless mannequins, she sat in the silence of her shop and ate her banana-flavored ice cream, spoonful after spoonful, until the white of the plastic bottom stared back at her, the cold morsels settling in her belly like dead weight, pinning her down.

Now, she moves toward the nucleus of the crowd to investigate its cause. People naturally step aside for the tall, unsmiling woman. In the middle of the human circle is a small man selling potions. "Solutions," he calls them. She hisses and starts to go away, shoving people aside, when she hears someone say to another, "Him say e be magician o. E go soon show us."

The word *magician* has made Felicity pause. There is a flapping in her chest that she doesn't understand. She turns back. It is her birthday after all; she can afford to humor a trickster. She looks around at the swelling audience, their eyes wide in anticipation. She shakes her head at their naïveté.

She pushes her way back to the front of the crowd and scans the wiry little magician. He is wearing a badly tailored white dashiki: threads dangle from the hem of the trousers and the blouse is too short for his torso, making him look even shorter. He is bald and his ashy lips combined with the smattering of bumps on his scalp give an aura of ill health. Despite this, he hops from foot to foot as he proffers his potions to cure cancer, treat erectile dysfunction, and bring home runaway husbands. His notice flits from person to person, his excitement matching that of his audience, who have left their shops to be entertained, as if he too will be amazed by his own acts. Felicity shuffles in impatience.

And then it is time. Felicity observes that he stows away his proceeds before starting his magic show, probably so that he will not be totally disadvantaged when things go awry. Smart, Felicity thinks. He introduces himself as Ayao and presents a low bow. He starts with a few card tricks. A member of the crowd picks out a card, a lot of skipping and dancing is done, and then he reveals the card—seemingly picked at random—to the exclamation and yelling of the people. They yelp in delight as he does this over and over. Felicity follows his moves, trying to uncover the charade.

Then a hush falls. It is time for serious business.

Ayao asks for a volunteer.

"For what o?" someone yells, and the people laugh. But she can hear the uneasiness pulsate in the air after their laughter has died down.

Ayao turns in slow circles to take in his captive audience. "To fly," he says.

There is a small, barely perceptible general step back. Felicity almost laughs. Almost. She sees Ayao's game: if everyone is too frightened to volunteer, the magician can feign disappointment and leave the market with his reputation intact.

So, she steps forward.

She can sense the crowd's surprise.

Ayao gestures for her to walk toward him. She does. He raises his left arm to shush the murmurs of the crowd.

"Do you believe?" he asks Felicity, his voice loud enough to carry over the crowd.

Felicity lowers her gaze so that she is staring right at Ayao. His lashes are long and bushy, emphasizing the size of his dark eyes.

"No," Felicity whispers, but in the quiet of the marketplace, it is just as loud.

"No?" Ayao asks, a sharp note in his voice.

"No."

Ayao moves away from her, step by step so that his eyes do not stray from hers.

"Do you want to drop your bag?" he asks.

"No," Felicity repeats, tightening her grip on the bag in blatant suspicion.

"Okay." Ayao walks back to her. He walks around her. He dances around her. Then he begins to chant, "Àṣẹ òrìsà l'ẹ́nu mi! Àṣẹ òrìsà l'ẹ́nu mi!" On and on, he establishes the deities he is invoking.

Felicity stands there—still, waiting for him to tire.

But he goes on, louder and faster. "Àṣẹ òrìsà l'ẹ́nu mi!"

Felicity has seen a man fly once. He jumped off the Third Mainland Bridge with his arms stretched out in front of him. As the people around her honked and screamed, Felicity had envied his freedom.

Then there is smoke, as there is in every tacky magician's show. Then people are screaming.

Why are they screaming? Felicity raises an arm to clear the smoke in front of her face. But her arm doesn't rise. Instead, feathers flap.

And now she is high above the ground, looking down at the market people running away from Ayao. The magician gestures for her to come to him. Ayao's hands rise to his shiny head, then lower, then rise again. He gestures toward her again, then turns on his heel and flees from a situation that's now out of his control. Felicity can see him winding through the streets.

Someone has snatched her bag in the melee but she doesn't care. She is far away from the chaos. She can now see a pattern to the rowdy market streets, and Felicity thinks how tiny the world must look to God.

And then she's off, because she cannot think of a reason not to go. The air here is so light and she is so buoyant. Felicity feels like she has been relieved of a lifelong burden of being. There is a buzzing echoing through her new tiny frame. Felicity is enthralled, riding on waves of air, her former weight forgotten, movement ruffling all her feathers—how they tickle, how delicate it all feels, precarious. How is she so weightless but still so strong? She slices through the air as she moves farther and farther from the market scene. She smiles. But there is no one to see it. Nobody to witness what it is for a bird to smile.

Felicity wants to see herself. She wants to observe her new form the way she did when she wore that long red dress. What type of bird is she? Is she colorful? Is she as black as the unhappiness that now seems foreign to her? She opens her mouth but does not recognize the warble that escapes. She knows nothing about birds.

Felicity heads toward a high-rise building with a glass exterior, jutting so far out of the earth like a challenge to gravity.

She starts to descend toward this building. Closer and closer, her reflection approaches her. She squints to bring the fuzz into focus. And then there is a boom. She has hit the glass, beak first. Pain jolts through her small physique in reverberations and the world goes black. Felicity feels herself falling and falling, and as she falls, she feels the heaviness of her being return.

When she crashes into the ground, she is completely Felicity again. She is engulfed in pain. She starts to weep. Do birds cry? When she tries to move, pain shoots out from her joints in waves. Her bones are broken.

Someone screams "Amusu!" and another yells "Àjẹ́!" Then there is a circle of people around her, calling her witch in their various languages. And she feels so weak, so weak and so tired. Blood seeps from unidentified gashes and she twitches with every fresh flood of pain. Now *she* is the show.

A stone smacks into her back and rolls to the floor, red with her blood. She realizes that she is naked. Other stones follow. The people close in; their fear chokes her—how does one fall as a bird and land as a woman? Their horror bites at her shredded skin like sand flies. Her old body feels weighed down, more than it has ever been, beneath their stones and their words.

A feather flutters into her sight and Felicity is reminded of her temporary weightlessness. She is in pain now, but she flew! She flew!

There are more voices and more stones but Felicity succumbs to the rising within her. Her body sinks further into the ground, but she is leaving it behind and rising and rising . . .

GIRLIE

MADAM SENDS ME TO THE MARKET THREE TIMES A WEEK.
Monday for household items, things like soap and Pampers. Wednesday for fruit and drinks. Madam drinks smoothies; Oga drinks beer. Friday for food: vegetables, yams, oil—but olive oil, not vegetable oil. "We're trying to be a healthy family," Madam is always saying. I never made smoothies before I entered this house. But I have learned many new things: like which buttons to press on the washing machine and how to iron with spray starch and how to pretend I am not sad or tired, even after fifteen hours of running after Baby.

Friday's list and money are waiting on top of the dining table that I polished this morning. They have such a big table with ten whole chairs when their family is only three people, and it's not even like Baby can sit in a normal chair, or like they have plenty of visitors. I look at the list and count the money two times to make sure it's enough. They don't do it on purpose, but sometimes there isn't enough money and I have to use all of Mummy's methods of pricing so that it stretches. Madam and Oga are not wicked people o; it's just that they don't understand that the way you know how much a car or house costs is not the same way you know that price of tomato can change before you blink once.

I put the money in the small leather purse Mummy bought me when I turned fifteen, eight months ago, before I left her in Akko, which is so far away that it's hard to believe it's in the same state. Akko is a village if you compare it to Madam's shiny neighborhood with smooth roads and houses that always have new paint. Mummy said I am a grown-up woman when she gave me the purse. I didn't tell her that I don't feel like a grown-up. I said thank you.

The walk to the estate gate is ten minutes and my uniform is already sticking to my back when I get there. Last month, the estate association said that okada and keke and colored taxi are forbidden from entering the gate. They are not thinking about all the people who don't have private cars, like the house girls, and lesson teachers, and drivers that have to drop their ogas' cars before walking to their own houses as far as Akko. If my load is too much, I have to take uncolored taxi back from the market. Mary and Abigail—who are doing the house girl program like me—have told me to do the sign of the cross before I enter any uncolored taxi. That they have heard of people that have been stolen, or robbed with guns, or even raped. I am not Catholic, but every time I have to enter one, I touch my head and my shoulders. I don't think I am crossing it in the right direction, but maybe direction doesn't matter to God.

The noise of the keke's engine reaches me, loud like pots falling down, before I see its yellow body shining in this wicked sun. When it stops, I enter.

◇ ◇ ◇

I BUY YAMS FIRST, two big hairy ones. Then I buy plantains. Baby likes plantains ehn! When I mash it and give it to him warm, his fat fingers will be swinging up and down in happiness. Every new thing I buy, I put in the basket that I rented from the annoying boys that are always begging everyone to use their baskets, running around and disturbing us like flies on going-bad fruit. My shoulders pain me more with every new thing I put in the basket.

The tomato seller is last on my list. Everyone calls her Iya Tomato. The woman likes me a lot. She's always smiling like she has won lottery when she sees me and adds extra tomato to what I buy. I don't have the heart to tell her that I cannot even have my own clothes in Madam's house, not to talk of my own tomatoes. Imagine! But I usually smile back while putting the extra tomato with Madam's own. Last last, it's nice when someone looks happy to see you.

Grace and Mummy Grace, who sell any kind of spice that you can want, are opposite Iya Tomato. Looking at them makes me think of my mummy. Mummy talks and talks when I call her. I just listen because I can only make one phone call a week and I know that she talks plenty to make both of us forget how she sent me to Madam. She says, "Girlie, do you know we still don't have running water . . ." and "Girlie, I entered one new supermarket and it was like entering freezer . . ." I listen and imagine that her voice is like warm ogi coming out of the phone, entering my ear and pouring around my heart.

I don't greet Grace and Mummy Grace today. I go straight to Iya Tomato.

"Ah, good afternoon, my dear." Iya Tomato's face is full and shiny. Sweat has settled on her round cheeks and they remind me of hot puff-puff. Maybe if I have change, I can buy puff-puff from the bus stop on the way back. But I don't want Oga and Madam to have even one reason to increase the time in my contract, or say that I have to pay the puff-puff money back, so I forget it. Iya Tomato's eyes are tiny but they are flashing, like a lantern is on inside her. She makes me shy with all her smiling, so I can't look her in the eye too long. She raises her hand as if she wants to touch my face, but returns it to her apron instead.

"Good afternoon o," I greet her back. "Please, two bowls tomato; one bowl tatase; half bowl onions."

But I know she won't sell until she has asked one million questions. She is always worried about me.

"My dear, how are you?" She moves closer.

"Fine, ma."

"Them no beat you? They treat you fine?"

I smile. "Yes, ma." I'm not lying. If Oga and Madam beat me, I can report to the agent that checks on me every month.

"You sure?"

A woman shouting into her phone accidentally hits me in the back. I move out of the way, closer to Iya Tomato's kiosk, and Iya Tomato has to step back too. It is a funny dance we are doing.

I say sorry with another smile. "Yes, I'm sure, ma."

Grace and Mummy Grace are laughing in their kiosk and I look to see why. Grace is holding her mummy's scarf in one hand so the woman can't catch it. Her mummy is saying, "Give it to me, o girl!" but Mummy Grace is laughing and covering her rough hair with her two hands. Their laughter squeezes something behind my eyes.

"And your mama, how is she?" Iya Tomato has never asked me this before, and I swing my head back to face her. Whenever anyone asks me about Mummy, inside my head starts shaking like washing machine just before it's about to finish. One time,

Madam asked me how I was managing, "a young teenager away from her mother," and I know that she was pitying me, but my head stopped working. I got so confused that I forgot to warm Baby's custard before feeding and he screamed and splashed it on my uniform. Madam has never asked again.

When Iya Tomato asks, I see red. I step away from her and mistakenly hit one boy selling carrot. The carrot boy shouts before arranging his wheelbarrow, hissing at me, then taking his fine orange carrots away.

I think Iya Tomato can see that she has scattered my brain with this question because she starts saying sorry sorry sorry. "My question is bad?" she's asking me. "Don't be angry, please. I bring your tomatoes now."

She spins to go inside her kiosk and her body is just doing gbim-gbim. She hits a carton of onions. Some scatter to the floor. She kicks them away as she disappears inside.

"Tomato, three bowl, abi?" she shouts from the back.

"No, two." My head is back to normal. I press my hand on my stomach. Let me just get these tomatoes and go back to Madam's house where I can think about Mummy all by myself.

"Ehehn! Farmers from the east bring new kind tomato. You'll take some to your madam, if she like, you buy next time? Come and see."

"Okay, ma." I drop my heavy basket under a broken table in front and follow her deep inside the kiosk, where the onion and tomato smells get heavier.

Iya Tomato turns to me when I am beside her. It is not bright as it is outside, but I can see her face is scrunched. Her eyebrows that are really just eyebrow pencil lines are pulling down and her nose is wide, as if she's inhaling all the air in the world, and I want to ask her if she is okay, if she is really breathing this way because of tomato? She raises her hands, and this time touches my face. I smell something strong on the dirty handkerchief she is holding, something I have never smelled before. Like cow shit mixed with flowers mixed with firewood. The smell travels fast up my nose to my brain, and before you can say "tomato," I have fainted.

◊ ◊ ◊

WHEN I WAKE UP, my head is pounding like it does when I have the worst menstrual pain. I don't know where I am. There are candles everywhere on top of Milo and Nescafé tins. There is a stool and a small table and a stand that they put the TV on, but no TV. When I try to stand, it is like my body is filled with water. Even my head feels like Baby is sitting on it. I can twist my head small, and I see that I'm lying on a flat mattress on a faded carpet. There is one door, but I cannot see what is after it.

A shadow appears on the brown carpet. Iya Tomato is beside the door. She is doing as if she's afraid to enter, playing with her hands. Is it not her house? Didn't she bring me here because I fainted? I need to get back before Madam thinks I ran away.

Iya Tomato comes closer and sits on the stool. She smiles and says, "My dear, you are with me now." There is something wrong with her smile and it puts fear in my soul. Oh God. I think I have been kidnapped. Mary and Abigail will never believe that it is a tomato seller, not some man in jalopy taxi, that can do this. I want to do the sign of the cross, but my hand will not come up. Iya Tomato's tiny eyes follow my body as if she is making sure I have not lost a leg or hand. I see she has thrown an adire wrapper on my legs.

"They no find you, no worry." When she laughs, I am left to look inside her mouth that is a strange dark pit. I have never looked at this woman for so long before. Her laugh is scaring me like mad. "No worry," she says again. "Nothing find you here, my girlie."

My girlie. Nobody else has ever called me that apart from Mummy. I want to throw my body at this woman and scratch her because she has no right. But I still can't move. Because she must have done jazz on me, one. And two, because it is not my way to scream and scratch. If I was that kind, maybe I would have shouted at Mummy not to send me away.

The mattress folds when Iya Tomato puts a knee on it to look into my face. She puts her sweaty hand on my cheek. "I teach you many things." Her breath stinks like onions. "Our people have forgotten all the good things of the ground. But I teach you everything the sisters taught me. We do everything together." Her hand strokes my cheek, like I am a dolly baby. "Like mother and child."

I wish I could enter myself over and over, make myself tiny, until my skin is not touching her own. She is not like my mother, God forbid! I don't want to learn anything from her, not things of the ground, not things from heaven.

Now she is saying that the first time she saw me, she knew I was the one. "You and me," she says, "we plenty alike. People abandon us go."

Nobody abandoned me. I am not like this madwoman. But even as I am writing *NO* in capital letters in my head, I am remembering Mummy crying in the street, I am remembering the contract, the paper that cut me.

I can count it on my fingers: seven months since I saw Mummy.

It feels like seven years, I swear. The day Mama Ngozi came to tell Mummy to consider the house girl program, I was waiting for Mummy to say no; to say: God forbid; to say: I can never let my child leave me to do house girl work. But she was listening and her eyes were stuck to the stove stain on the wall. Mama Ngozi said everything was formal. Apply, do training, go to family, get paid. Straightforward business, not like the old days. She said we should not listen to the people on TV calling house girl work slavery, that this one would be like office work. I waited, but Mummy was quiet. Me too, I was quiet.

That day in the House Girl Center—the agent calls it HGC—Mummy was holding my hand like she wanted to squeeze all the blood out. In my other hand, I was holding the biro they gave me like I've never held biro in my life. The biro was heavy like metal. The agent man with his dirty nails pushed the paper for me to sign. The side of the paper cut my hand. I was looking at the thin line of blood that looked like red thread until he cleared his throat and I wrote my name in my handwriting that is crooked like chicken scratch because it has been long since I went to school. After I signed, it was like NEPA took light inside my body.

Time to go; Mummy was crying so loud and there was catarrh everywhere. She kissed my forehead with all her tears and I think that the tears were a kind of blessing. After that day, when I'm sad or angry, I touch my forehead and it feels like Mummy is close and I calm down. Before I entered the car that took me away, I just repeated the words she said to me before: *It is a good plan.*

Now, Iya Tomato says, "Don't cry! I have scared you?" I didn't even know that I am crying; I can feel nothing. Her voice is going up up, but she is talking to her own self, touching her chest. "Every time, every time! The girl is scared now." She faces me with a new smile. "I will sing to you. Like my own mama used to do."

She closes her eyes and moves her hand to my shoulder, smoothing my gray uniform up and down. Her singing voice is different from her talking voice; it's the kind of voice you can find on radio. I don't understand the language of her song. I look away from her and concentrate on the yellow bathroom slipper under the TV stand that looks like it belongs to someone ten years old. I don't want to listen, but her song is making me lose my thinking and I am fighting it and fighting it until I can't fight again. A breeze from nowhere tickles my eyes and softly softly, I fall into sleep.

◊ ◊ ◊

I MET MARY AND ABIGAIL at the training center where they took us for one month. They did not look sad to be there. Mary said house girl work is better than ashewo work, which her auntie who raised her was doing. Abigail nodded but did not say anything about where she came from.

HGC taught us many things. How to carry a baby. How to be close, but not too close, to your employers. How to complain if your employers beat you. How to manage being away from your own family. How to discourage oga from making eyes at you. We practiced with fat baby dolls and knelt to greet the trainers, who were pretending to be ogas and madams. I listened hard because I wanted to be a good house girl so that Mummy would be happy and we'd have money and I could go home. And part of me was hoping that if I worked very hard and worked on all my off-days, then we wouldn't have to wait two years before I could go home. But it doesn't work like that.

Only two years. Then, one year and nine months. Then, one year and five months. The number keeps reducing, but so slowly, and Mummy reminds me when I call her that our plan is to use the money to start a proper business that is not stationery business, a good business that will bring money fast, maybe hair salon. She said, "I go save half of everything for us, my girlie. The time go just pass fast, okay? We'll pay rent for fine house and find you good husband and we'll be happy!"

I don't really care about fine husband and tall house with paint and smooth road and 24/7 water and light. I just want to be at home beside her. I was nodding my head at her plans even though, deep down, I was feeling betrayed the way she said she felt when my daddy disappeared when she told him she was pregnant. One time I said, "I want to come home," and she was quiet for so long that I thought the phone had gone dead, but I heard she was crying. "Isn't it for both of us?" is what she asked me. "You can't do it for us?" But her asking that question is like me asking Baby if he wants to eat after I've already pushed the plantain inside his mouth. I don't like to think about it because I really love my mummy and she really loves me.

Before, when we were still selling envelope and padlock and notebook and biro together at the post office, I used to like writing my name over and over on old envelopes. Mummy would tell me stories when the radio battery died, while we prayed for more people to come to the post office and need envelopes.

The story I remember the most is about a boy and his mother. This woman and her son worked every night and day on their small farm and they got just enough food to eat between them. They ate the yams and tomatoes and corn from their farm. They were all each other had in this whole wide world. One day, the mother fell on the farm, her body squashing the vegetables, her body burning like kettle on fire. The boy carried his mother home. He fed her agbo and all the leaf medicine he could find. But the mother was still hot hot hot. He cried on her feet and his tears were cool on her dry skin. When he had no more tears, the spirit of the forest came to him and said, I know how your mother can get well. The boy said, I will do anything! The spirit said, Are you sure? There is a plant at the end of this earth, but you have to fight strong animals through the biggest, thickest forest, and climb the highest mountain and swim in the deepest sea, and if you live, then you will find the plant to cure your mother. The boy jumped up and said, I will go now! He kissed his mother goodbye and went to look for the plant.

When I asked Mummy what happened after, if the boy died on the journey, she was doing her face like my question was stupid. "That's not the point ah," she said, looking away from me to someone entering the compound. "Customer! You want buy envelope?"

◊ ◊ ◊

WHEN IYA TOMATO SINGS and I sleep, I have a dream that Baby is blue and dead and Madam and Oga call the police and the people from HGC and they say I killed Baby. They call me a witch. And Mummy is there too in my dream, crying, and she is shouting: Oh, my girlie, what a waste! And the HGC people pull the contract out of my hand, and they leave me holding blood and they leave me and Mummy holding none of the money they are supposed to pay.

Iya Tomato comes through the doorway when she hears me crying. "Stop your cry. Talk to me."

"I need to go. Baby needs me." My body is pressing flat like she has stapled it to the mattress.

"Nonsense!" Iya Tomato laughs something harsh and all the fat on her neck shakes like jam. "They have finished controlling your head, my girlie! They don't need you. I'm sure they have replaced you by now. You just another gray dress to them."

I am not! Madam likes me. Her voice is soft like my bed that is the softest bed I have ever slept on in my whole life. And Oga is kind to me. Sometimes he nods that I can finish his chicken when I am packing the plates. And I love Baby. He makes me tired, but I like to hear him laughing and saying nonsense in a language he alone can understand. I eat in Madam's kitchen after I have finished feeding Baby; I like the quiet time. I am starting to see that it is good sometimes when you know what you're getting from somebody and everything is straightforward, like Mama Ngozi said. I clean and cook and Madam sends money to the agent who sends 85 percent to my mother. She is not changing rules anyhow, like Mummy or Iya Tomato. And although Madam touches my shoulder in a soft way sometimes, I remember the HGC teacher shouting "This is strictly business" so loud that some of his spit landed on my hand.

"With me," Iya Tomato says, "no work, no gray dress. We live happy." She leaves the room and comes back with a cup, handing it to me as if she doesn't know that I don't trust her. "Roots, leaf, seed. Taste."

Because I have no real strength, she captures my head and pushes the thick liquid through my lips. I close my throat but I need to breathe and it goes down. A trick that I have used on Baby before.

I am afraid to faint again, but what happens to me is so strange that if I describe it to anybody, they will say I am telling fairy tales. When the liquid that is thick like pap touches my stomach, it's as if I have touched live naked wire. My whole body shakes. My toes become warm, then that warm feeling starts to travel up like a snake through my legs and thighs, and when it reaches my stomach, it makes noise like when I'm hungry. It climbs my chest and throat, and when I open my mouth, laughter comes out. I swear, I don't understand. I am in this crazy woman's house and I am sad and I cannot even move my body, but I open my mouth and it is such fine laughter, like all the wishes I have ever wished have come true.

Iya Tomato is clapping the way Baby claps when he is watching his cartoon of the cat and rat. This strange woman says to me, "See? Don't you like the feeling? Don't you like it?"

IT IS NIGHT WHEN my eyes open. I don't want Iya Tomato to know I'm awake, or she will start talking nonsense about being mother and child again. My feet are in her lap. I can see her putting a towel into a bowl of water, then rubbing it on my feet. It is so gentle, the way she is rubbing my legs, and I did not even remember that my legs have been paining me from seven months of running after Baby. It feels nice.

When I lick my lips, it is as if I am still tasting that happiness. Is this not jazz, is this not magic? Or is there something about roots and leaves the rest of us don't know about? Mummy says magic is bad, even though it is in the stories she tells me. If something makes you happy, can it be bad? This woman looks so happy to be washing my dirty feet. Can it be so bad to stay here and have her take care of me since that's what she wants so badly—badly enough to steal me? I am tired of fighting.

I think she knows I'm awake, because she starts to talk. She does not look at me, or stop wiping my legs. She tells me a story. Her own is about a mother and daughter that sold things in the market. One month, ankara; dried fish the next. After some time, their business stopped going well. Nobody was buying from them. The mother and daughter tried everything, but when nothing worked, they cried, holding each other. Then the mother heard about how some people got help from the oldest tree in the forest. The mother left the daughter sleeping at home and went to visit the iroko tree in the middle of the night. The tree saw her coming and laughed. Another one? Yes please, the mother begged, help me and my daughter! And the iroko said, Bring me your daughter for a month, and your business will grow again. But the woman said, No, she is all I have! The iroko laughed again, a laugh that sounded like thunder. The tree said, I give you three days to decide. The woman went home, her shoulders bending in sadness. She held her daughter. Three days went, and the woman and her daughter were hungry and their bellies made noises like forest animals. Then the woman told her daughter what the iroko wanted. The daughter cried and cried. But they went to the forest anyway, and the iroko brushed her daughter's hair and pulled her close with its branches. The mother went to market and business was good. When one month passed, the woman missed her daughter so much, but she said, Let me wait just one more month so we never have to go back to beg the iroko. But when she went to the forest after the third month, she could not find the tree, or her daughter.

"Whenever thunder strike, the woman will look to the sky,

then cry in the middle of her plenty money and food, and the woman thinks the thunder sound is the iroko laughing at her."

When Iya Tomato finishes the story, my tongue is swelling inside my mouth and I am afraid that it will fill up my whole head, and when you look in my ears you will see pink. I gather all the strength inside me to remove my legs from her comfortable lap.

◊ ◊ ◊

ANOTHER DAY PASSES AND all I can taste is anger, and loneliness. I wonder if Madam or Mummy is looking for me. Even if I rub my forehead, I know I won't feel Mummy and feel better.

"Enough!" I say to Iya Tomato. "I want my mummy!"

Her face turns tomato red and angry. "Your mummy?" Her voice is so high it is like a nail stabbing my ears. "I show you secrets of ground. I make you laugh like baby who never see trouble. And you still cry for mummy? See this one!" She is throwing her hands about like she wants to fly, and all this movement makes one candle go out.

I have noticed that when she is getting angry, she starts talking to herself. If she did not make me so afraid, I would be laughing. Now, she is breathing fast and clapping her chest, saying, "When you no think well, bad things happen. Calm yourself." The funny thing is that it actually works. She comes to kneel in front of me, calm. Never has a grown-up woman knelt in front of me like this. "See, think well, my girlie. If your mama really love you, why she send you to work? Small girl like you should be playing on street. Mothers not suppose do that." That onion smell again. "Mothers suppose sacrifice. If people see you here, if they know that I take you, I can go to jail. If the sisters find out, they will be very angry with me again. But I make that sacrifice because I love you."

My eyes are tied to the candle that went out. My skin feels like bad spirits are in the air.

"Girlie," she says, "have you ever been so lonely that you want to die?"

The answer is, *Of course yes, every day since Mummy sent me away*, but I know she doesn't want a real answer, like the way Oga asks "Have you seen this economy?" when he is reading morning newspaper.

Iya Tomato continues, "When I get belle for my stupid boyfriend, and my mama and papa send me away out of shame, that was me. So afraid and alone, girlie. I was walking on express as if trucks were made of paper. I was so ready to die. But one day, this woman pull me from the front of danfo, she saved my life and asked my story. That's how she introduced me to the sisters. They are all market women, too, but special ones who know the secrets of the ground. It is secret group, but they could see my pain, my alone, and they took me in and took care of me like I'm trying to take care of you." She touches my ankle. "They teach what to put in soil to grow fat tomato, how to make drink that can cure fever in one hour, even how to punish the stupid boyfriend that was pretending as if my baby was not his own. It was good to have power that I have never had before. You understand?" She looks into my eyes, then away. "When my baby came, I was happiest woman in Nigeria. Sisters are good, power is good, but the baby was the best. My own personal person. Life complete. But when my baby get sick—small cold—I think I have more power than I actually have. Before I even ask my sisters for help, I try to cure my baby with my own hand. Big mistake. One night did not even finish before my baby—" Iya Tomato's voice is sad with tears that don't show on her face. "My baby die before morning."

She is looking like she stole something from me and she wants me to forgive her. Me, I am now feeling sorry for this woman who is alone, like I am alone, and who only wanted good things for her baby. We all make mistakes. Even me, I have done things I shouldn't do, like eating Baby's food or burning Madam's dress with the iron and pretending it was a mistake. Or like pinching Baby one time when I was missing Mummy and he would not stop crying. Even Mummy made a mistake when she sent me away. All bad things. I am starting to see Iya Tomato is just a sad woman who has kidnapped me, and maybe she regrets it the way I regret those things I have done. Her face is even starting to look different to me: the way her forehead is high and shiny, the way she is always twisting her hand in her lap as if she is still a small girl on the inside, the way she blinks two times instead of one time like a normal human being.

"It's okay," I tell her, even smiling a little bit. "It's okay. I promise not to tell anybody that you kidnapped me when I go back."

"Go back where? What are you talking?"

She frowns. I frown.

"We are together forever," she says. "I have all this plenty love that is choking my heart, my girlie. I will give it to you now. All of it. We will be happy. You are my baby."

When she says that, all my soft feelings explode into something very ugly and stinky. "I am not your baby!" I shout at her, so it can get into her thick skull. "Your baby is dead!"

Iya Tomato slaps me. The surprise makes it more painful. I don't remember the last time anyone hit me. My eyes have found that yellow slipper again that is too small for Iya Tomato's big leg, and scary things rise in my mind, like, What if I am not the first girl she has kidnapped from market? Didn't she say that her sisters would be angry *again*? My face is stinging like one hundred mosquitoes are biting me. I am thinking, if I even try to leave this woman, she might kill me first. What if she does to me whatever she did to her bad boyfriend? If her roots drink could make me happy like that, why won't she able to cause me plenty sadness? Maybe she even put that rubber slipper there as warning? I am thinking: I am in real trouble.

◊ ◊ ◊

THE DREAM I HAVE this time is actually something that happened, true true. From before. I am sitting between Mummy's legs and my shoulders are warm where her thighs are pressing me. Mummy is twisting my hair. She always did my hair and it always made me feel like my love for her can drown me. Virgin hair cream smelling everywhere, thick. I like the way Mummy's hands are heavy on my head.

I ask Mummy what will happen to her if I die.

She says I should not think about that. That a child is supposed to bury the mother after the mother is very old.

I say, "But Gabriel died and his grandpa buried him." Mechanic Gabriel was the grandson of one of our old neighbors, and he died of pneumonia because the grandfather did not have money for hospital. The last time we heard of him, the old man was pushing his hand into people's faces, begging for money because there was no Gabriel to take care of him.

"That one na unlucky death," Mummy said. "You no be Gabriel. You no dey go anywhere. I no dey go anywhere."

If I was a small girl, I would have just nodded and said okay. I am not yet a grown-up woman, but I am not a small girl still sucking her finger that you can just say "Don't worry" and I will stop worrying. That thing with Gabriel really shook my spirit so whenever I saw someone begging, I would run back to Madam's house and mop faster and scrub harder. I wanted to work hard so that Mummy would never feel like she has no child, like Gabriel's grandpa. Even when Baby vomited in my face or my back was doing like it would break, or Oga looked at the food I cooked like it was rubbish, I did my best.

But as I am lying here in Iya Tomato's house, trapped, I am thinking, What is even the point? Am I sure Mummy will not say I should go back and work for another two years after my contract with Madam and Oga has ended? If she is not missing me now, will she even remember me after two years? Mary said her auntie said she would stop prostitution after their money was enough, but she is still doing it. Because, can money ever really be enough? The day I asked Mummy about dying, she said, "You no dey go anywhere; I no dey go anywhere," but she was not telling the truth because I am here. Everything might be different if Mummy just asked me first about the HGC contract. "Girlie, do you want to go?" Or if Iya Tomato just asked me whether I can be her friend that is like a daughter. Because I am starting to feel like one of Baby's toys that cannot even say yes or no. Is this what it means when you are a daughter?

Iya Tomato brings yam pottage for me to eat. She puts her hand at the back of my neck, as if I am a baby, so the food can enter well, and I remember the way Mummy used to feed me when I was sick. Maybe when I make my eyes small, Iya Tomato's small eyes can become big like Mummy's own, and her neck can become slim like Mummy's own, and maybe I can trick my head into thinking she is Mummy.

"Mummy," I say. To say the word is like to swallow hot agbo. No, it is like to spit hot agbo out of my throat. The word is bitter and hot and immediately after I say it, it is like I have been attacked with sore throat. I cough and say it again, "Mummy."

Iya Tomato stops putting food in my mouth. She drops the bowl to the ground and looks at me hard, and I think her eyes are beginning to grow wide, wide like Mummy's. At first, she bends her head as if she is not sure what she has heard. But I say it three more times—"Mummy, Mummy, Mummy"—and her eyes are shining like that lantern has come on again inside her. In a strange way, I think she is very beautiful now.

Me, I am thinking of another story. But it is not a story I heard from Mummy. It is not a story I heard from Iya Tomato. I heard it on the radio one afternoon when Mummy left me to sell envelopes on my own. Or one day when I was looking outside Madam's kitchen window, cleaning snails with potash. Or I heard someone tell another someone in a keke napep. It is a story about two children, a boy and a girl. They have daddy and mummy. But because they do not have any money—it's always money, every time—the mummy and daddy send them into the forest to die so they will not have to think about food for the children. In the forest, they find an old woman's house and she says she will take care of them. The woman gives them food and bed. But the girl is sure that the old woman is just feeding them so they will become fat and tasty for her to eat. When the woman tells the girl to check if the fire is hot, the girl pretends like she doesn't know how to push firewood, and asks the old woman to teach her. The old woman and the little girl who is not yet a grown-up woman stand in front of that fire, watching each other.

I have been thinking very hard, but I don't remember what happens at the end of that story.

"My girlie," Iya Tomato is saying, and I close my eyes. "Oh, my girlie! My girlie!"

WHEN IYA TOMATO BRINGS me a pink dress to wear, I push my hands through the sleeves. The dress has flowers around the neck and smells like sweat, but it is exactly my size. I cannot lie, it is nice not to be wearing the gray uniform, but I cannot forget the yellow slipper, or who has been wearing this dress before me. When Iya Tomato asks if I like the dress, I say yes.

We go deep in the bush when the night is dark, so dark that if you tell me to take you back to where we have come from, I will not be able to. She makes me hold her hand so I will not fall. Her hand is big and warm. I don't know if she is thinking about me falling or if she is afraid that I will run away. The day after I called her Mummy, my head stopped feeling like Baby was sitting on it, and then after another day, I was able to stand up from the bed. My legs were shaking because they had forgotten how to work, and I hugged her and put my head on her big breasts and I said, "Thank you, Mummy."

When we finally stop in the forest, she releases my hand. She waits awhile before she brings out a lantern and lights it. What I can see in the new light makes my mouth open. I have been in bushes before, but the ones I've seen did not have trees like this that are so fat that you will need seven of me to hold hands before we can make a circle around one; they did not go up so high that if I try to find the top, I might break my neck; the leaves were not this green that it looks like what is in Baby's cartoon. This forest is a wonderful place that smells like rain has just ended, like everything is soft and happy. No wonder everyone puts it in their stories.

I look back at Iya Tomato, and even in the shadow I can see she is smiling as if the way I am looking at everything has made her happy. She puts the lantern down and kneels. "Come," she tells me, putting her hand soft on my leg. "Come and learn the things of the ground. I will teach you what the sisters taught me."

I kneel beside her and the ground is like cushion under me. Iya Tomato is pointing to this and that, saying, "You see the way this stalk has four baby stalks?" and I am listening to her tell me the name of everything and I am somehow happy to be learning the secrets of the ground. But at the same time, I am not looking. The corners of my eyes are seeing the darkness around us and I am thinking that anything can happen.

I can run into that darkness.

But maybe not today. Maybe after we come to the forest many times and I learn what root and leaf to put together to make happiness move like snake through the body, then I will also learn what root and leaf can make a big woman sleep deep, and it is that time I will run.

Maybe at that time, I will not want to run, maybe I will love Iya Tomato and her scary kindness toward me, and I will think she is my real mummy and even love her weird blinking. Maybe I will stop feeling hot agbo in my throat when I call her Mummy.

Maybe I will have forgotten my real mummy then, forgotten her face and forgotten her voice and forgotten the way she used to kiss my head and plait my hair. Or maybe I will always remember her, and when I run away from Iya Tomato, I will go to Mummy and she will beg me to forgive her for sending me away and I will tell her everything as we are hugging and crying, as if she can ever believe this Iya Tomato story.

But maybe when the time comes, I will think that I am tired of being anybody's girlie, and I will go somewhere nobody knows to call me "girlie," or to ask me where my mummy is, or whether I even have a mummy, and they will instead ask me what my name is, and I will be able to choose a name and my own story, a story that I am making up by myself.

THE WONDERS OF THE WORLD

ABISOLA FOUND HERSELF SITTING NEXT TO THE NEW
boy, Zeme, because she was the last person to board the bus. A
day ago, she hadn't thought she would be joining her classmates
on this geography excursion. Her mother was suddenly able to
afford the trip when some Alhaja stumbled upon her shop and
bought forty yards of Swiss lace. So, this morning, Abisola's
mother stood at the back of the school bus, pressing cash into
the hands of the trip coordinator, Mr. Baju, while Mrs. Korede,
assistant coordinator, manned the door of the bus, waiting for his
decision. The payment deadline had passed a week ago.

Abisola watched, off to the side, as Mr. Baju surveyed the
crumpled envelope in his hands. She looked away when his pitying eyes slid from the envelope to her, down to the oversized
sneakers she'd borrowed from her father. When Mr. Baju gave
in, she let herself be hugged by her mother, then pushed her feet
against the backs of the shoes, closing the gap, so nobody else
would give her that look.

Inside, Zeme was whispering to nobody, his hands steepled
under his chin, eyelids closed. Abisola leaned away from him,
into the hard plastic of the armrest that prevented her from falling

into the aisle. The first day Abisola saw the new boy on the school grounds, she had thought of spaghetti. Zeme was all wriggly and lilting. His waist cocked to the left, then swayed to the right. He waved his hands in front of his face when he spoke, a music conductor, his own voice the song. Every sentence was high-pitched and keening as if searching for the perfect key, a crescendo rising to a climax that never came. She noticed how he made people uncomfortable; all that looping and undulation. She resisted the urge to reach out to him, prop him up, keep him steady.

But there was something else that prevented this contact. Something Abisola's mother would call "nervous energy," what their music teacher would call his "aura." The boys in their class simply said, "That dude freaks me out." That *something* made Abisola feel exposed whenever Zeme looked at her, as if he knew all her secrets and was only keeping them out of a condescending benevolence.

"What are you doing?" she asked of his steepled fingers, still angled away from him. She was curious, but her real motive was to trade seats so she could have the window.

Zeme's lips paused. He raised his head. The bulgy eyes that had already earned him the nickname "Froggy" opened to locate her. His lids slid against muddy brown irises, then he asked if she wanted the window. She nodded yes, only slightly startled at his intuition. Behind them, similar switches were happening.

"You like the billboards?" He hadn't moved yet, his whole body still, except for those eyes that wandered her face. Abisola fought the impulse to spread her fingers in front of her nose, hide herself from him.

Yes, she liked to look at Lagos's billboards with the slogans written in pidgin. She enjoyed hating on the ads, sneering at the exaggerated grins on the magnified people. Did the MTN man advertising one month of free app downloads really have to smile so hard that it looked like his face would split? She didn't believe in his happiness. She couldn't relate to that joy. Abisola wondered, though, if she would get a new sense of self if she were blown up ten times her size, lifted high above a city of twenty-one million people.

To Zeme, she shrugged. He stood then, plastering himself to the row in front so Abisola could take his seat. An image of a lizard came to her, a particular one she had found high on her bedroom wall one Saturday morning, staring at her. When they settled, she repeated her question.

"Praying," Zeme answered. He flexed fingers and cracked knuckles. She cringed at the harsh treatment of his frail-looking digits. "I'm praying," he repeated, the *y* in the word sustained, a held note. "There's a long journey ahead of us. And my people say I'm a prophet."

Abisola stopped talking to him then. She nodded, that slow bob of disbelief. She turned to look out the window, at a billboard. TASTE AND SEE, WE GO SCATTER YA BRAIN! a seasoning cube promised. But at what point had brain scattering become a thing to entice people with, Abisola wanted to know; at what point had having no control over your mind become a desired thing? She rested her crinkled forehead on the cool windowpane.

◊ ◊ ◊

HER SS3 CLASS WAS HEADED to Ikogosi to see the confluence where the warm spring met the cold spring but didn't mix.

"Why do they call you a prophet?" Abisola asked Zeme when the bus stopped for a bathroom break close to Ibadan.

The other students noisily spilled out of the bus at a Mr Bigg's parking lot, into the arms of squawking hawkers who waved everything from bread loaves to bananas to kuli-kuli to boiled eggs in their faces. The students contorted and twisted free of the traders who grabbed at them, running the rest of the way to the eatery's doors. Mr. Baju trailed them, dodging some ripe bananas thrust in his face. He had asked the students to submit their phones to him, to be returned on the trip back. "No distractions, talk to each other!" He was bringing his zealous classroom energy to the excursion, Abisola thought; he began every Tuesday/Thursday class with a cheesy icebreaker, calling the rocks and rivers they studied "wonders of the world." She thought it was a little sad, a little naïve, how he wore his excitement on his face, in front of teenagers who saw any kind of earnestness as weakness.

Abisola and Zeme lingered in the bus. Something they had in common at the moment was aloofness from the other classmates. Zeme, because he was the new boy who slithered around school, his gaze the only steady thing about him. Abisola, because she had recently turned down the advances of one of the school's popular kids. Musa was one of the tall, fine boys that other girls reapplied lip gloss for, whose parents owned a house in London. After she said no to Musa, the other boys began ignoring her in solidarity, and Abisola wondered if the girls were affronted that she would reject someone they pined for, believing this to be an indictment of their tastes, or a show of superiority.

It was neither. She was interested in Musa, his tight Fulani curls, that slash in his eyebrows; but the fear of a time when he would want to hang out on the weekend, or visit her at home, was too much. Would she invite him into their two-bedroom flat where the lonely chairs skidded across the chipped terrazzo floor;

where the door to the kitchen had no handle so they had to stick a finger into the hole and jerk-jerk-jerk until it came unstuck? And underneath this shame was a murkier fear, not yet articulable to her; something about dividing what very little happiness you had between two people. Abisola was glad he wasn't in her geography class.

"Sometimes I can see things that are coming." Zeme's head leaned on the seat in front, his voice wafting toward Abisola. "Other times, I can stop what's coming. I don't know if that's what a prophet is, but that's what they call me anyway. Ever since I was a boy."

"Things like what?" Abisola's parents were not religious; they refused to join the "seeking poor of Nigeria," those who went from church to mosque to shrine, looking for a miracle, for a panacea, for hope. "Tsk-tsk," they would go, clicking away from a church's broadcast service on television, "when will they see there's no answer there?"

Zeme turned to her. "Okay, so a while back? My dad's first wife from like a million years ago suddenly started calling my mum all the time, out of the blue. She said my mum was the reason they broke up, that she had a vision where my mother was a mountain in her path. It was very stressful. Then, one night my mum wakes up feeling like she's dying. She said her throat was closing, her head was light, her spirit was trying to leave her body. So, she comes into my room and says, Zeme, pray for me. I had been awake already, unsettled, like I was waiting for something that I didn't know yet. I held her until she felt better. In my arms, I could, like, literally feel her body calm down. And I felt so tired after the whole thing. You know, like Jesus after the woman with the issue of blood touched his garment? Anyway, when we woke up the next morning, we heard news that my dad's first wife had died mysteriously in the night."

Mr. Baju knocked on the side of the bus and Abisola jumped. "We're not stopping again o! You kids better go get snacks or use the toilet now."

Hawkers swarmed the two potential customers when they got off the bus, Abisola squinting at the back of Zeme's head, running the story again through hers, weighing it for truth. A man wearing a dirty yellow Lipton cap was selling Gala, his carton of skinny sausage rolls braced on a shoulder. He started to approach Zeme, who was a head taller than everybody, even with his leaning and slanting. Then the Gala man froze. Abisola saw it all: the fear that stretched across the man's face like a mask, his eyes growing wider and wider, filling out his face, as if he were looking at a dead cousin that he put in the ground himself. She saw Zeme stiffen mid-stride, turn to the man. It was then the Gala man let out a small cry, like a woman during her first contraction, startled and strangled and sharp. The man lifted his Gala box, turned, and ran in the opposite direction, kicking up dust and gravel, nothing on his heels.

◊ ◊ ◊

AT THE IKOGOSI RESORT, Abisola was paired with Dania, a girl in SS3C who wore an oversized wristwatch—signifier that she had a boyfriend—that kept sliding off her wrist. They entered their room in silence and Abisola picked the bed Dania didn't. She pushed her bag under it and sat, taking in the tie-dye curtains, the framed cliché of a dark-skinned woman with a calabash on her head. There was another photo of an Egungun masquerade dancing against a black background. The masquerade's form was bulky but graceful, something eerie about a possessed man in weighted cloth spinning so high above the ground, the patterns on his colorful garb blurred by speed. Her eyes moved to the ankara runner on the small fridge, the wooden mask sitting beside the lamp on the dresser. It was one of those resorts that catered to foreigners, visitors they had to assure this was "the real Africa" by creating everything out of unpolished wood, carving tribal marks and symbols into every surface.

Dania walked up to the mask and turned its long face down. "Not ready to have nightmares," she explained, her first words to Abisola.

Abisola didn't have nightmares, but many nights she couldn't sleep because of the pressure in her chest. It started slow, her heartbeat increasing steadily until it was bursting through her ribs, knocking in her ears, stealing her breath. She cried on those nights, the darkness outside crowding in, the world closing in. It always started in her bed, and yes, she was tangibly conscious of the fact that she was lying on her thin, flowery sheets and her too-flat pillow, her parents on the other side of the cheap stucco wall; yet she was also viscerally convinced that she was floating in a galaxy, alone in the black ink of the universe, a loneliness crumpling her whole body into a tenth of its size, squeezing.

Her father would wake up to her crying, come into the room, and lift her trembling teenage body into his arms, transferring her to lie between him and his wife. Some nights, the contact of her parents' sweaty bodies was enough to calm her heart. She would hold tightly to their arms, digging in and bruising skin until she could breathe again, tension draining from her muscles and leaving hiccups behind. But other nights, even the weight of their hugging arms wasn't enough to quell the terror that darkened her sight, the certainty that she was absolutely alone in the middle of her life and couldn't be reached by anyone.

Her parents were hoping the strenuous activities of this trip would knock her out every night. She was to request her phone back from Mr. Baju if she had an episode. Abisola surveyed Dania, who was laying out her swimsuit, sizing up what her roommate's reaction would be if she were to scream herself awake, sobbing. She did not want to find out.

"You're getting close to that Froggy boy, abi?" Dania asked when Abisola continued to watch her. She smoothed out an orange strap, then swung her hand back up to catch the imitation Rolex before it slipped off.

Abisola shrugged. One of her fears as she trailed Zeme into Mr Bigg's was that this would further push her away from the rest of her classmates. One doesn't become less of an outsider by befriending the other outsider.

"You should ask your new friend why he is changing school one term before we all graduate secondary school. Ask him why he left his old school."

Abisola sat up straighter. "Why? Why did he leave?"

Dania laughed and looked up to meet Abisola's eyes. "Ah, no o! Me, I don't gossip."

◊ ◊ ◊

ABISOLA HAD BEEN in a different school once too. She spent her first two years of secondary school there. But one day, she came home weeping. She knelt in front of her confused parents, begging not to go back. No, nothing had happened to her. No, nobody had touched her, bullied her; she wasn't failing. She just couldn't go back. Whenever she stepped into the school premises, her head felt double its size, her body double its weight, and she dragged from class to class, sinking into the floor. She was sure she would die if she went back. Her parents had shared a look, but the next day, she was walking into her present school to take an admission test. They could not afford the new school, they even owed school fees at the old one, but her father said that no thirteen-year-old should experience such despair. Abisola never forgot that afternoon her parents sprang into action for her, into action and into debt.

That was some three years ago. Whatever had brought Zeme here, Abisola did not need to know. They were here; this was now.

◊ ◊ ◊

THE CLASS DROVE AN hour west to climb up Erin-Ijesha Waterfalls the next morning. Mr. Baju said he was saving the Ikogosi confluence visit for last. "Be careful!" he kept screaming as they climbed the stone steps, interrupting his own long speech about how marvelous the seven floors of Erin-Ijesha were and how it was a shame that the students were too lazy to climb to the seventh plane, which housed a village.

"There's a story about a catfish that was caught here a long time ago," he said, clearing his throat. "That when they tried to cut it up to cook for the king, its head kept growing back."

"Na so!" one of the boys shouted, imitating a cough. The others laughed and Mr. Baju joined them, his chuckle weak. Abisola turned away from his humiliation.

"Of course," the man added, "it's only a myth. No science there."

Zeme was behind Mrs. Korede, and Abisola watched his arms spread out on either side for balance. He lifted his nose high in the air, as if imitating that *Titanic* scene. His body rocked left to right as if the wind were his dance partner, the drum of the waterfall in the distance an accompaniment. Abisola moved to catch up with him, one foot gingerly in front of the other because these borrowed sneakers made her feel even more unmoored than usual.

"You people need to believe more things," Zeme said in a singsong voice when she caught up with him. His *s* sustained itself and she recoiled as if he were hissing at her, warning her. But then he turned to bare his mouthful of teeth in a grin. Was this about Mr. Baju's catfish story? She slipped a little and focused on her feet.

Safe at the waterfall, Dania eagerly stripped down to her orange swimsuit, pulling her T off in one swoosh. The others followed her lead. Zeme peeled his shirt off, then his shoes. His ribs indented his skin with every breath and Abisola tried not to wince. His back curved sharply when he sat next to her, his spine a crooked *C*. She removed her shoes and hugged her knees to her chest on the rock they sat on. The waterfall beat against a jutting rock and the other students took turns standing beneath it, to be slapped by the torrent, crying out in delight. Mr. Baju started to ask questions about what they knew about these rocks, but Mrs. Korede touched a shushing hand to his shoulder and he fell silent.

"Poor Mrs. Korede," Zeme whispered, and then plunged his feet into the water and giggled a high tinkling sound. His toes squirmed in the shallow water and Abisola saw they were painted. A deep forest green that matched the algae on the rocks. She could not look away from those skinny toes that danced beneath the clear water; the color green seemed to become more vivid the longer she stared.

Alive. The laughter of her classmates faded away along with her sense of reality, and the color loomed so she felt pressed up against the algae, the roughness of rock scraping at her skin, the brightness of its color blinding her. The wet air grew denser and Abisola struggled to breathe. Her heart throbbed in her ears as if she were underwater. Everything melted away there in the daylight, every person, the water, the trees, the rocks—all blending into an amorphous threat. She was alone again, drowning in green. The distance between her and Zeme was the span of many planets, the expanse of lifetimes.

When Zeme touched her thigh, he crossed that gap and Abisola was no longer alone. She sucked in a deep breath and coughed hard until her chest hurt. Her tear-filled eyes sought out Zeme's. Abisola didn't understand what had brought on this episode; she had slept through the night without interruption, nudged awake by the light that filtered through the tie-dye curtains to warm her face. Now, this, happening in broad daylight, canceled out the relief she felt in the morning.

But perhaps this episode happened so Zeme could see. He was witness, and she didn't shy away from his appraisal. She pressed down on his hand, attempting to communicate the heaviness through skin. "Help me," she said, her voice raspy. "You say you're a man of God. Can you take it away?"

Zeme's nose flared at her plea, but that surprise was almost immediately replaced by a shade of victory in his smile. Behind his head, Abisola caught Halimat, one of Dania's popular friends, frowning at her; she had just stepped away from the waterfall to wring water out of her waist-length braids. Halimat's gaze moved from Abisola's face to the hand grasping Zeme's on her thigh; then she raised her brows. Abisola yanked her hand from under Zeme's. Flustered by Halimat's continuing stare, she lowered her chin to her chest.

◊ ◊ ◊

ABISOLA WANTED TO BE HAPPY, for her parents. She saw
the way her cousins laughed with a lightness that was foreign
to her, creating dance routines to entertain their parents, even
into their late teens, gossiping with their mum about all the
weirdos in school, making tea for their father. They once put
salt in his Lipton as a prank, and his bellowing laughter continued to ring in Abisola's head for the rest of that holiday, a
mocking reminder of the joy she was not giving her own father.
And yes, Abisola was sure that a part of this levity came from
wealth; her cousins' house in Ikoyi was big enough to host all
the relatives every Christmas. But even in her own household,
Abisola watched from under hooded eyes how her mother tick-
led her father while he cut paw-paw on the deep freezer—how
she took his finger into her mouth when he inevitably sliced it
that day, how they laughed and laughed outside her bedroom
window when her father pulled the generator rope so hard that
it snapped. They stiffened when she entered a room, soberness
congealing their features. They didn't know they were doing it,
but she saw every bit lip, flexed jaw, their concern for her casting
a shadow over everything.

Maybe Zeme could help her become one of those lit paper lanterns she saw in *Mulan*—a bright floating presence in their lives.

◊ ◊ ◊

ON THE WAY DOWN from the waterfall, Mrs. Korede fell and
twisted her ankle. There were several accounts of what happened. Dania then Soji then Halimat shouted over each other,

clamoring around Mr. Baju, gesturing in his face. They claimed to have seen Zeme push Mrs. Korede. Eli and Wale insisted no, they had seen him reach out to prevent the fall. All the others steered clear of the argument.

Abisola had been trailing the group, wanting to put distance between herself and what she thought was an embarrassing outburst for help at the waterfall. The group crowded around the fallen Mrs. Korede, still dripping. Mr. Baju tried to cut the yammering short by lifting a hand.

Mrs. Korede's teary face moved from person to person as they argued above her. It was well known among the students that she was easily swayed, that a good argument and strategic tears could bump a grade in her English classes. Abisola once overheard Kovie, the Youth Corper, teasing Mrs. Korede about her long "Deeper Life" skirt suits, and she suspected this was the reason for Mrs. Korede's cellulite-baring short shorts that Dania and Halimat had been snickering at. Now, as her head moved from student to student, their arguments rising again, Abisola could see the English teacher failing to settle on someone to believe. When asked directly what happened by Mr. Baju, she stuttered and lowered her head to inspect her scraped shin and swelling ankle.

Through all this, Zeme sat next to the woman on the ground, watching the blotchy ankle grow in size. Every time his name was mentioned, either in defense or in accusation, Zeme twitched as if stung. He looked in the direction his name was coming from, then back to the ankle. He leaned into Mrs. Korede and whispered in her ear. She startled, then relaxed. When she bent her head toward his chest, eyelids lowered, Abisola knew he was praying again. She studied the ankle from the gaps between bodies, waiting for something, anything, to happen to the ankle, which looked exactly like skinless uncooked chicken.

Mr. Baju clapped and the group turned to him, silenced. "John, Soji, assist Mrs. Korede. The driver will meet us by the fruit sellers. Let's not throw accusations around willy-nilly."

Halimat rolled her eyes, but they all obeyed. The boys helped Mrs. Korede stand on her good foot. She let out a whimper, then bit it down. John was the school's star basketball player; he could lift her without help if he needed to. He nudged Zeme aside, but Zeme did not flinch, just unfolded himself to an upright position.

Abisola did not watch him; she watched the ankle. The whispers continued and Zeme trailed the group this time, hands folded against his belly. Abisola did not go to him; she was paying attention. She watched Mrs. Korede limp, limp, limp, supported by both boys, but by the time they neared the fruit stands, only John was holding onto her. She placed weight on the twisted ankle cautiously, then with more sureness. She extricated herself from John's bulk and rotated the ankle. "I think I'm fine," she said. "Thank you, John. Looks like it was a small thing."

The whispers stopped for a moment and everyone gathered around Mrs. Korede for the second time. Halimat stooped low to survey the ankle, waiting for it to expose Mrs. Korede's words as a lie. The swelling was gone. Nobody looked at Zeme.

"Well," Mr. Baju said. He clapped once. "Well!"

◊ ◊ ◊

WHEN ABISOLA STEPPED OUT of the room in the middle of the night, unable to sleep, she was not surprised to find Zeme seated in the shaded courtyard. The night was quiet and humid.

Abisola sat next to him on the cold cement slab and shifted forward so her bare thighs did not touch concrete where her shorts ended. The palm trees joined in Zeme's whispering; crickets provided backup.

Abisola shivered. Zeme did not acknowledge her presence. She squinted around at the puzzle of lit windows, wondering who was in whose room. Dania had stumbled into their room around midnight smelling of weed, a full two hours after they had been dismissed by the teachers for the night. Abisola had absently traced the girl's path to the other bed, wondering what respite her own parents back home were experiencing in her absence.

"Are you praying again?" she asked Zeme. She removed her feet from her slippers and pulled at the damp grass with her toes. "Did you do it? Did you push her to show us that you could heal her?"

Zeme stopped whispering. He sat up straight.

"We have one more night," was all he said, and Abisola knew that if he didn't help her before they left this place with the trees and the springs and the crickets, it wouldn't happen. She would be marooned on the island of her life, unable to meet her parents, unable to meet Musa, unable to meet anybody who offered her any kind of happiness.

"Well, okay?" She moved closer to him, leaned in to search his long nose, his thin lips, those bulgy eyes.

"They didn't believe." He let out a long whistling sigh. "I just wanted to make them believe."

"Them?" Were there other classmates he'd been trying to convince of his power? "Are you talking about us or your old school?"

"Who's there?" Mr. Baju's voice whipped out of the night from the door of his room on the upper floor, saving Abisola from the details. "Zeme Imoh? Abisola Lawanson, is that you?" Mr. Baju's voice sounded panicked and Abisola jerked away from Zeme, understanding how the scene could be interpreted. "What do you think you're doing here?"

Zeme and Abisola stood.

"If you don't get back to your rooms! I'm watching you . . ."

Abisola jogged to her room and closed the door quietly behind her; but as she slid into bed, Dania's voice came out of the darkness. "You don't hear word, you this girl. You don't listen, abi?"

Abisola ignored Dania and closed her eyes, fantasizing about a girl who looked just like her, bent over laughing hard, laughing so hard that her heart knew what it meant to burst out of her chest for all the right reasons, for all the bright reasons.

She lurched when she felt a clammy palm on her arm.

"It's just me," came Dania's voice again, now beside her bed. The faintly acrid smell of weed came with her. "Calm down, ah." Then, in a softer decibel than Abisola had ever heard from between her lips, "Can I sleep beside you? That blaze messed me up. Dunno where Hali got it from."

Abisola sat up; a light sweat from the fright coated her forehead. She faced Dania in the dark.

"Please," Dania added. "I'm seeing weird shit. That mask is not supposed to be moving. Please."

Abisola shifted and Dania got in beside her. They lay side by side for a moment, staring at the ceiling. Then Dania contorted so that her head was touching Abisola's shoulder, warm breath tickling her cool arm. Abisola breathed out all her tension and focused on the point of contact, skin on skin. She closed her eyes. She slept.

◊ ◊ ◊

"YOU REMEMBER OUR CLASS on this? A confluence is where two or more flowing bodies of water meet and then run together. But see here, the warm spring meets the cold spring but they don't mix? They glide on, their own separate paths!" Mr. Baju's voice boomed over the pallor of the group. It was their last full day, but the students all seemed in dour moods, as if they had been given bad news. He kept turning to Mrs. Korede, his imploring gaze enlisting her to contribute, to elicit a response from the somber group, but she was slumped against a rock herself, staring at a couple holding hands while dipping plastic bottles into the warm spring with their free hands. "Did you know," Mr. Baju asked his students, "that some people believe the warm spring has healing properties?" Nobody responded. The couple filled their bottles and walked away without glancing at the school group.

Abisola had woken to find Dania absent from the room. She had apparently gone to get ready with Halimat. On the trail, Abisola waved at her, but Dania refused to look at her or leave Halimat's side. Zeme was quiet too, standing still in a way that was more unnerving to Abisola than all his swaying and winding. She wanted to push him, restart his motion. Everyone looked so glum. What had the night taken from them? Something shifted in the air and unsettled Abisola's stomach.

"You've probably heard about the myth of these springs?" There was a queue to step into the water; the other confluence visitors chatted and took pictures, but the excitement did not extend to Abisola's class. "That there was a hunter with two wives?" Nobody stirred. "One wife was very quiet; the other was very troublesome. They argued all the time. One day, they went to their husband for him to settle their fight and he cursed them and they turned into these springs. Who can guess which wife is which?"

Nobody took Mr. Baju's bait.

When it was their group's turn, they climbed down to enter the water in pairs.

"Be careful! Put one leg in the warm spring, and one in the cold spring, and be stunned!" Mr. Baju's voice was nearing a screech, but when the first pair of students entered, neither admitted to being stunned.

"How can you not marvel at God?" Zeme's mellifluous voice piped up, and Mr. Baju's head whirled. Zeme was talking to no one in particular, just letting the words out of his mouth to fall over them like mist. "You know the first people to acknowledge and organize around this confluence were some Christians? A small Baptist church that eventually sold their land to the government?" Zeme blew air through his teeth; it came out as a tune. "You could say this is holy ground."

Abisola watched Mr. Baju's jaw work. She wasn't sure if it was because he hadn't in fact known this, and resented Zeme for flaunting his knowledge, or if it was more about Zeme's religious tone when their school was proudly secular. She thought her geography teacher looked violent for a moment. Mr. Baju shuffled backward, away from Zeme. He bumped into Halimat, who hissed and sidestepped him. "And what does this have to do with geography?" he asked, eventually.

"Everything, Mr. Baju," Zeme said, and then it was his turn to step into the water.

John was supposed to go in with Zeme; he was the closest. Abisola skipped and slid forward to grasp John's arm. "Hey, can I go before you?" John shrugged and stepped aside.

Zeme stretched his hands out to Abisola. She took them and stepped into the water with him. The water soaked the bottom of her shorts but barely went halfway up Zeme's shins. Cold, then warm. She curled her toes.

"The warm spring is about seventy degrees, while the cold spring is thirty-seven." Mr. Baju's voice was louder, as if he were saying an incantation. "But they don't mix, they don't mix! Isn't that amazing?" A startled Mrs. Korede eyed him, wary of this burst of spirit.

Abisola closed her eyes, her hands still within Zeme's grasp. The warm water was warm. The cold water was cold. Who cared if they mixed or not? If she engaged every atom of her person, if she sent all her weight toward her feet, would her burdens be swept away with the tide? Would she step out, an untethered balloon? Oh, to float home on the tropical winds and knock against their window, have her parents open up and take delivery of their new child, their new Abisola who would be luminescent with giggles, effervescent, buoyant, joyful.

Nothing happened.

Abisola opened her eyes. Zeme was smiling at her. Was he mocking her? She yanked her hands out of his, betrayed. With Mrs. Korede's ankle and the Gala man and that look in Zeme's eyes, had she only seen what she wanted to? What had she really hoped for? Tears clouded her sight as she spun around, lost her footing. Down she went. Then Zeme's hands were there; she felt them, like fish, scaly, or rubbery, and they were groping for her hands, her arms, pushing her further away from the water's surface. Abisola started to lose her breath. She wanted to thrash; her body was telling her to flail, to make it known that she was losing air, swallowing water. Her head lightened. Water moved against her and filled her up, but it was distinct from the heaviness she felt on those nights that she could only weep.

Abisola coughed out water when she was hauled from the springs. She drew in long breaths that cut pain through her chest. She cried harder. She felt robbed.

"What is happening? What is happening? Is she okay?" Mr. Baju's face appeared above Abisola's. His forehead furrows mirrored waves. Then Zeme's face replaced that image. His eyes were so bright, as if he had just witnessed magic. "How do you feel?" His mouth was now by her left ear; his breath smelled like grass after rain. "I baptized you," he said. "How do you feel now?"

The thing Abisola knew about baptism was that there was a submersion, then a lifting up. But she had not wanted to be lifted up. She had been weightless under. When Mr. Baju said, in that myth, that the man had cursed his wives, he must not have understood. How was that a curse? Abisola wanted to be water too, to be light, to flow despite gravity.

◊ ◊ ◊

ABISOLA GOT TO TALK to her parents. She was given her phone and guided to her room by Mrs. Korede, who rubbed her back with solid strokes that calmed her hiccups. They moved away from the loud voices crowding Mr. Baju insisting, again, that Zeme had been the cause of this event. This time, Mr. Baju's gaze swung from person to person, looking unsure and frightened.

"Baby, what's wrong? What's wrong?" Her parents' voices pooled in her ear, so warm and worried, and Abisola knew that she had failed again. A weekend away from home and here she was casting shade on what should be a breather for them, a holiday from their albatross.

"Nothing, I just wanted to say hello."

They weren't buying it. "Your voice is all cracked, have you been crying?" her mother wanted to know. "Bibi, you know you can tell us anything, should we come get you?" her father offered.

"No, no, I'm fine. I fell and I cried, but I'm fine now, I promise. I'm fine." They had the phone on speaker and Abisola heard her words echo in the room around them.

"Are you hurt?" Their voices were a chorus, and their unity in this small moment made her tears well up again. Would she ever flow with them, be part of the chorus of their small family; or would she always be the odd one out, off-key, their strange child weighing on their lives with her sadness?

"No, no, please don't worry about me. I just wanted to hear your voices. I begged Mr. Baju to give me my phone for five minutes."

They were silent and Abisola could imagine the exchange of looks that would be happening over the phone. "Okay then. We'll come pick you up tomorrow from school. Three p.m., abi? The car broke down again but we'll borrow Nkem's car or something."

"Okay." Abisola rubbed her forehead and mud came off on her hand. She wiped it on the bedsheet.

"We love you, okay?"

"Okay, bye."

"Abisola?"

"Yes?"

"We love you, okay?"

"Okay." She breathed out and her laden heart shed some of its weight. "I love you too."

◇ ◇ ◇

DANIA FOUND ABISOLA STILL in her wet clothes, staring at the mask that housekeeping had righted.

"Abisola?"

She didn't respond, but Dania moved till she was within Abisola's field of vision. She waved. "Hello-o?" When Abisola still didn't answer, Dania sat on the bed but stood as soon as dampness touched her thigh. She squatted instead and manually turned Abisola's head toward her.

"Look, Abisola," she said. "That Froggy boy, he convinced this guy in his old school that he would see perfectly if he broke his glasses. Like, he was performing a miracle and all the boy had to do was believe. The poor boy that was almost blind . . . he did it, broke his glasses that were as thick as Coke bottles. Then he fell down a flight of stairs. It's true. Halimat's boyfriend goes to that school and everyone was talking about how the gullible boy broke his leg and neck. The boy's using a wheelchair for now."

Abisola blinked.

"I'm not lying!" Dania mistook her silence for disbelief. "Froggy's parents took him out cos the students in the school started being super mean to him and he would just be quoting the Bible at them, talking about signs and wonders and saying nothing else, and it was all very weird, but like, the boy's parents couldn't do anything cos the boy took off the glasses by himself, right? You can't really say Froggy forced him. But it's all weird, all

very weird business. There were other things, like he was laying hands on people and conducting deliverance services during free class periods?"

What gorgeous eyes Dania had, Abisola noticed for the first time. They were wide apart on her face, almond-shaped. She had a great face for billboards, smooth and brown and beautiful. Her eyes would twinkle from the heights and the people would buy whatever she was selling.

"Okay, whatever, be like that." Dania got up in a huff. She made a clatter throwing her box open. She pulled out another swimsuit. This one was red and white, striped. "We're having a party at the pool. Mrs. Korede will be there, she's convinced the Baju to leave us alone for a while." She pressed the swimsuit against her stomach. "You can come if you want. You should."

At the door, she turned again to Abisola. "He pushed Mrs. Korede. I saw him, I swear."

Abisola returned to staring at the mask. She nodded. She believed.

◊ ◊ ◊

ABISOLA WORE HER PLAIN black swimsuit and threw on an oversized Wema Bank T-shirt she'd plucked from her parents' wardrobe. It was from when her father worked at the bank, before the downsizing, before their family moved out of the duplex into the other flat, before this smaller flat. It smelled of wardrobe, of disuse, not her parents, but she didn't mind.

At the junction with the wooden arrows showing directions to the pool, confluence, restaurant, main office, Abisola turned toward the confluence. Her rubber flip-flops slapped against the

wooden dock. At each bend, there was a rustic lone bulb hanging from a stick and wire. She kept going. A bird called, another answered. A fly buzzed around her cheek and she lifted a shoulder to brush it away. At a corner, she heard the fizz of laughter drift toward her on a wind that smelled of oranges. She kept walking.

At the steps down to the confluence, she found Mr. Baju seated. He looked up at her approach. "Lawanson?" He squinted, raising a hand over his eyes. "Abisola, is that you?"

She moved closer so he could see. "Yes." A few steps away from him, she stopped and leaned against the wooden railing. She hadn't expected to meet anybody here. The railing was rough underneath her skin. There was a smog over the springs, but she found the current.

Mr. Baju returned to staring at the water. "They call those unity trees," he said, and Abisola looked to the two trees by the confluence. One was a palm tree, its bark rough, the other had a smooth stem.

Abisola nodded. It was in the resort's pamphlet.

"Zeme Imoh left. He said he had to leave immediately and his parents arranged for a taxi to pick him up."

"Ehehn?"

"Yes." Mr. Baju sighed. "Probably for the best. He's a weird one, isn't he?"

Abisola thought about it. "I think he just really wanted people to believe." Even now, she didn't think of the pressure of his hands underwater as cruel. He had seen her. He had wanted to help.

Mr. Baju frowned at her but didn't respond.

A wind blew and ruffled the trees, the branches whispered a prayer, the springs gurgled a song.

"Isn't it fantastic that they don't mix?" His voice was soft, the

kind of soft that comes before or after tears. "I just wanted you kids to look at this marvel and feel a tenth of my awe. They don't mix! What a wonder. Isn't this a wonder?"

Abisola felt a wash of gratitude for his presence—an echo of her parents, whom she would soon be reunited with, wrapped within, different from, but connected to. She listened to the springs coexisting side by side, retaining their own virtues, stubbornly separate at their meeting but gliding forward together, bracing each other, bound forever. "It is," she agreed.

THE DUSK MARKET

THERE IS THE SMOKY SMELL OF DRIED STOCKFISH, THEIR rounded bodies flush against each scaly other, glinting gold, all impaled on slender sticks blackened from fire. There is the buzzing of protective flies that circle the bloody cuts of meat: lamb shoulder, turkey breasts, cow thigh, ponmo—chopped cowhides curling into their rubbery selves. There is the singeing heat from the agbada, frying yams and sweet potatoes in the large cast-iron pan that can fit four small children. There is the ringing of tiny bells and the thrum of voices; the sung invitations by sellers, the gruff bartering of buyers, the undercutting whiny complaints about humidity and noise and prices. But before all of this, it is the flicker of flames within rusting kerosene lanterns that will show you the way to the dusk market.

On the way home from work, pedestrians stall at this intersection, they pivot on weary heels, deciding to take the long route. Drivers speed past this stretch of road. They are not sure why, but feet press determinedly down on the pedal once they have passed the corner of Faleye and Ororo. Breath is held, hands tighten around the wheel, leaving stripy impressions on palms. If a child says to their parent, "Mummy, why is that man hopping on his head?" or "Uncle, that big bird is winking at me," they are ignored.

The women of this market are just like the women you know. Mama Ibeji who sells okra and ugwu, has the same smile as your landlord's wife, the dark shadows between gapped front teeth drawing the gaze. Mummy Keji, grinder of spices, has the limp of your office cleaner, the left foot slapping down, the right sliding up to meet it. Iya Tunde's shoulders dance when she's charming a buyer to her bottles of palm oil: shrugs punctuate sentences, shimmies emphasize enjoyment, and these shoulders hike up when she feels affronted. Just like that woman who's always at the newspaper stand.

No, these market women are not women you know, but they could be.

When the sun slinks away, when the light of the day thins out—oranges replaced by dark grays and purples, the women come out of nowhere. Their wooden stalls are laden, threatening to buckle under the weight of their wares. Their yarn lantern wicks are raised and lit.

With the women present and the lanterns burning, the market stretches beneath their feet and comes alive.

◊ ◊ ◊

YOU DON'T SEE THE dusk market if you are not invited to the dusk market, but there are slippery moments, slits, frissons. It is when this happens that the children see hopping heads or winking herons or stray dogs dancing like humans, front paws slicing through air gracefully. If an adult happens on this quirk of time and chance, there is a bokeh of yellow light at the periphery of their vision, a streak of blurring neon when they snap their heads to catch something that isn't there. Left with that unsettled feeling, that bitter taste at the back of the tongue when afflicted by malaria, most don't dare look a second time.

But Salewa does. After she ingests a quarter of her remaining ogogoro, the locally fermented and distilled spirits she sells to bricklayers and area boys, Salewa's eyes are willing to see more than is otherwise available to her. She walks really slowly in the direction of this intersection, this stretch of road, her inhibitions dulled, her instinct to run away melted into a puddle of sputtering signals.

In Salewa's basket, the reused glass bottles knock against each other as she makes slow progress to this road that she would not usually pass. She is singing a song to herself, a lilting ballad of love and time and beauty. Salewa believes she has none of these, a thirty-six-year-old woman with breasts that sag, sharing a room with five other petty traders in a building that has no bathroom. She came to Lagos on the back of a ram-transporting truck, twenty-one years ago, and she has been on her own since, her life among the bricklayers and agberos sometimes echoing that seven-hour trip between the curly horns of smelly animals. Salewa is a lonely woman, an alone woman who knows her survival is based on hiding this fact.

The warble of her song is accompanied by bottle clinks, and the melody tinkles into the deserted street. The bokeh of lights appears at the corner of her right eye and Salewa shakes her head, all drowsy, gin sloshing in her brains. She blinks and trudges along. Her dirt-crusted slippers accumulate more mud on the unpaved sidewalks. When the lights flicker again, Salewa stops and turns. The song collapses in her throat. In front of her dilated pupils, the lights tighten into focus and Salewa sees.

She sees the lanterns first, rows of yellow dots disappearing down the street, glass bowls stained brown from the lick of flames. Then she sees the goods: catfish splashing in shallow bowls, bristly tubers of yams propped against each other, piles of ugu leaves, grain pyramids of garri and honey beans. Behind the goods, the women materialize in colorful patterns of ankara, headscarves twisted carelessly, wrappers hanging precariously off waists. They call to each other, they embrace, one woman's head on another's shoulder, another's arms circled around a thick waist. The buyers come last, their backs to Salewa, shadowed, moving from stall to stall, lifting a mango here, prodding a tomato there.

Salewa sees the dusk market appear around her, and she hears its sounds next. Her face flushes, her basket slips from her fingers, and just when she acknowledges the warmth in her belly, this goo in her heart, this desire to stay in this strange, dimly lit market forever, she blinks and the empty street is once more laid before her, its barrenness taunting her.

◊ ◊ ◊

THE NEXT DAY, Salewa cannot concentrate on selling her bottles. The image of the dusk market is beginning to fade from her memory and she wonders if it was all a dream. She forgets to call out to the conductors at the bus park and only her regular clients find her, jostling a knee, calling her back to earth.

She measures the sharp-smelling spirits distractedly, years of this trade making her unconsciously precise. She nods when they pay, tucking the proceeds between breast and bra. She smiles abstractly when they tease her, gauging her interest to go home with them, go behind a bus stop shack with them. "Sali-

Salewa, you know I'll bring heaven down to this earth for you."
"Salewa-my-loverrr, na me and you foreverrr!" She smiles the
right amount at their red eyes and chemical breaths, the stink of
days-old-sweat-meets-weed on their clothes; just enough smile to
get a tip—an extra fifty naira, but not enough for them to mistake it for real interest. Their promises are nothing; more about
the libations held in her bottles, the ability of the liquids she sells
them to make them forget the hardships of Lagos and the indigni-
ties of their labor, more than her, her real self, the inside Salewa.
She learned this the hard way in her first couple of years in this
wild city, giving too much to men who lived lives that held on
to nothing.

But forget these men, their syrupy tongues, their slimy hands
that can break a heart, a body. It is that market Salewa wants, the
soft light, the pleasant hum of commerce, that warmth of cama-
raderie she had stumbled unto, into, for a short moment or two.

She leaves her perch at Ajajogbon bus stop and wanders
toward the adjacent retail market. The shops here are made of
brick and mortar, storefronts hosting Caucasian mannequins
clad in traditional dresses or crude handwritten signs advertising
for help or perilous towers of raffia baskets, leaning. It doesn't feel
the same to Salewa. She squints at the corners between shops,
the dark alleyways connecting the identical bungalows that make
up the market, but she sees no mysterious shadows, no hazy yellow lights.

"Wetin you want?"

Salewa has unthinkingly stopped in front of a brocade store,
obstructing the entrance. The salesgirl who has asked the question is young and beautiful, silver braids framing one side of her
face. She glances at Salewa's basket of spirits.

"Ehehn?" she continues when Salewa doesn't answer.

"Nothing."

"Then comot for here. Go! You're blocking our customers."

Salewa shuffles a little to the left, her eyes lingering on the shimmer of the braids, the way light bounces off it.

"You still dey here?" The girl is sneering at Salewa's basket now—red-coated lips angling up, at Salewa's muddy feet, the faded iro circling her waist. "Madam Ogogoro, abi you don lost?"

And Salewa thinks about this question as she moves away with a shrug—shame is no longer a close friend of hers. She furrows her brow and she thinks and she thinks. Lagos is so big. Is anyone ever not lost?

◊ ◊ ◊

THE SUN IS ALWAYS high overhead, burning the scalp lines between plaits on Salewa's head. When the sun goes down and she has finished selling the day's bottles, she must go find the market. She unrolls her headscarf and spreads it over her head and shoulders like a cloak—to protect her from the sun, like a tent, amplifying her isolation in the midst of the bustling pedestrians, the evangelizing preachers, the bus drivers yelling for passengers.

Salewa watches the danfos crawl in and out of the park, spitting exhaust in her face. In the middle of waving a cloud of smoke away, she sees a face in the melee she thinks she recognizes. A face from twenty-something years ago in that tiny village so far away from Lagos, where she rode bicycles on dirt roads and jumped into the river naked with her friends and drank palm wine from her father's cup when he was passed out under the guava tree.

The face is older now, lined around the lips, but that bulbous nose is the same, one eye still bigger than the other.

Salewa finds her feet and walks toward this woman, this visitation from her past. "Derin!" she calls out, bumping against swearing passersby. "Aderinsola!"

The woman pauses, her eyes darting around for the source of this call.

Salewa tugs at her elbow, recoiling when her palms leave a streak of dirt on the woman's white blouse. Now, she notices the white blouse. Now, she notices the gold necklace. Now, she notices the woman's tightening grip on her purse.

"Aderinsola?" Salewa wants to confirm. But it is her; she is sure.

"Who are you?" the woman asks.

"It's me, Salewa. Aren't you daughter of Baba Aribigbe and Alhaja?"

"Who are you?" the woman repeats, her mismatched eyes squinting now, taking in Salewa's hair, her iro and buba, her black and scaly feet.

"It's me, Salewa," she repeats. "Remember Baba Sule? The mechanic? Na my father."

"I don't know you," the woman says, beginning to turn away.

But Salewa does not believe her. It is Aderinsola with the nose and the eyes, the one who ran away to the next village for one night with a singer, flogged by her mother all morning when she returned. Salewa is absolutely sure it is Aderinsola. They weren't friends, but she was there when the background of Salewa's life was not just opaque strangers, but real defined people with lineages she could trace and stories she recognized. She was from the life Salewa left behind, the life before someone showed up and convinced Salewa that Lagos would give her more than the village could offer.

"I don't know you," the woman repeats, a new bite to her words. Then she scurries away, her high-heeled sandals inappropriate for the uneven ground of the park.

The retreating woman is immediately swallowed by more moving people, busy people, hustling people, city people.

◊ ◊ ◊

WHEN SALEWA RETURNS TO her basket, of course it is gone. She doesn't even cry out, what is the point? After all these years, shouldn't she know better than to let her guard down? It is her fault, chasing ghosts in a city like this. "In Lagos, every man for himself," one of her former lovers had drawled to Salewa when she asked for a loan to start a different business. "God for us all!"

Now, Salewa is in trouble. She will have no money besides what is in her bra for the rest of the week. What she should do is go to her distributors, beg them to give her bottles on credit, then work through the nights for the next month, trying to make it back. What she should do is start working on a moving, believable story to tell her landlord come Sunday. But instead, this further unmooring—caused by losing her livelihood tools—has strengthened Salewa's desire to see the market today. It is urgent now. Somehow, she believes her life depends on it.

She leaves the bus park, hanging on tightly to the dregs of yesterday's memories, led on only by the glowing dots in her mind, the greens of the vegetables, the market women swatting flies and beckoning with the same hand.

When Salewa gets to the corner of Faleye and Ororo, she sees nothing. There is a street, but nothing else. There are no pedestrians. Every once in a while, a car will come sputtering by, fracturing the eerie silence, speeding past until it merges into the cross street. Salewa walks the length of the street. She spins around sharply, as if to catch something unawares. There is nothing to catch. She cries out, a keening thing. She walks the path she has just walked again. There is a shoddily paved road, potholes and speed bumps punctuating it every other meter. The sidewalks are unpaved, dirt holding onto the last rainfall. On either side of the road is unbuilt land. She walks up and down the street and Salewa finds nothing, sees nothing.

At the next junction over, Salewa asks a woman roasting corn about the night market on Faleye and Ororo. The woman barely looks at her, fanning the coal under her corn and ube with a colorful hand fan.

"Nothing dey that street," she tells Salewa. "No market. You mean Ojodu Market?"

No, Salewa shakes her head. She walks away from the woman and on to the next roadside makeshift market where women and young boys sell fruit in wheelbarrows and metal trays. They don't know either. "You're sure it's not Alade Market?"

No, Salewa shakes her head. The fruit sellers feed on their own produce, spitting seeds in the gutter. "Isn't that the street the governor wanted to build big plaza that year, where their foundation kept collapsing and collapsing?" someone asks, and others nod, remembering. "There's no market o. Whatever spirit dey for that street made sure nobody goes there."

Salewa buys an orange, thanks them, and continues her journey, stopping anybody, with increasing randomness and compulsion, stopping everybody. The market with the lanterns and the women? But her descriptions could be of any market, they point out to her. And why can't she just go somewhere else?

"Ah, me I don't do night market o," some say to her, drawing out the sign of the cross—forehead, middle of chest, shoulders. "I hear that it's spirits that sell in these markets."

And others say, "Night market? God forbid! I hear it's spirits that buy from night market. Abi, are you a spirit?"

Salewa looks down at her calloused hands, her ashy skin, her clothes heavy with dried sweat. No, she doesn't think she is a spirit. But how is a spirit different from an unrecognized body, a body with no connections, nothing tethering it?

◊ ◊ ◊

THE PINKS OF EVENING are seeping into the sky and Salewa is tired. Her back hurts, her ankles ache. Wasn't it all a dream? Is she being stubborn to insist it wasn't all a dream? Just like the specter that is Lagos, bright and glittering from a distance, nothing but grime and sweat up close.

She buys a small bottle of alomo bitters from another ogogoro seller. She glares at the woman's half-empty basket in envy. She chugs it down, slapping her chest at the bite. The bottle lands on a pile of rubbish with no sound. She makes her way back to the street where she maybe saw a market with golden flames and wooden stalls that braced each other up. Alcohol has always made her stubborn.

There is still no market. The sun lowers and Salewa does too, onto the pavement. A car or two starts to slow down when they see her, but no, the street is still unsettling to everyone else. She wishes she had her spirits with her. The alomo in her belly is begging for company. She is not numb enough. This hurting defeat in her chest is too sharp. She sits for a while in the waning afternoon sun, breathing shallow.

"Excuse me, ma?"

Salewa looks up to see a young girl wearing tight jeans and a crop top that exposes her belly.

"Yes?" Salewa's head tilts back further to take her in. She is tall and skinny, except for that stomach, and is holding onto what looks like a heavy bag. "Are you lost?"

The girl frowns, shakes her head, then nods.

Salewa is tired of craning her neck, and the drink has made her heavy. She returns her heavy head to the cradle of her palm. "Can I help you?"

"I don't know."

Salewa shrugs at this response. How can she help someone who is not sure they need help? "Yes?" she prompts the girl.

"Maybe, ma? I'm looking for work?"

"You're looking for work?"

"Yes ma! I just come to Lagos. From middle-belt side. I'm ready to work hard here."

Salewa wants to laugh, but she can't make it come out of her. Instead, a smelly burp escapes. She looks down at her basket-less hands and notices she is still holding onto the single orange she bought from the fruit sellers. How many years in Lagos, and nothing but an orange and some worn naira notes smushed against her breasts to show for it.

"My dear," she says to the girl, "you fit go back?"

The girl comes around to stand in front of Salewa. "Ma?"

"I say go back. Nothing dey here."

"I can't. My uncle suppose pick me from that bus park last week, take me to his house, but he never show."

Salewa understands the man who didn't show up. The thing about Lagos is that you are embarrassed to go back, or embarrassed for the people who knew you before to realize that your move to the big city has earned you nothing. Welcome to disappointment, she could say, but she invites the girl to sit next to her. The girl lowers her bag and sits on it.

"Lagos is hard," she tells the girl. "Sorry about your uncle."

"But I will work hard and Lagos will work out fine. Na wetin my uncle talk."

Salewa stares at the big toe on her right foot. It is black on the inside. "How old are you?"

"Seventeen."

"Ah."

"But if I work hard, it will be okay?"

Salewa doesn't want to lie, but she also doesn't know if anything would be different if she had been told the truth those many years ago, if she had been warned of the loneliness that would plague her days and nights, the years she would wander in the hot sun, her skin turning to leather, the hard work that would yield nothing because everything is stacked against you, that she wouldn't remember the last time someone, who wasn't a drunk client, called her name.

"What's your name?" she asks the girl now. Sometimes, when you're drowning in this sprawling place, just another addition to the million hopefuls streaming in daily, hearing your name can be what makes it feel a little like a home, even if only for the duration of your name's syllables.

"Nengi."

"Nengi," Salewa repeats. *"Neeeen-giii . . ."*

"What's your own name?"

"Salewa."

"Okay. Auntie Sha-lay-wah, what can I do?"

Salewa doesn't answer. Her eyes follow the setting sun. She watches its slow descent. She has not looked at the sky this way, has not watched the sun set since she was a young girl lying by the river with her friends, spread out naked on their wrappers as late as they could go before their mothers started looking for them. Salewa has not watched the sun set with anyone in so many years.

The colors are not quite orange, not quite amber, not quite red, constantly shifting, trying on new intensities and hues as the clouds drift across. She watches the self-illuminating ball go down, the dark blues and purples streak in, staining the sky as it morphs from day to dusk. Salewa watches it all and Nengi watches it with her.

"I don't know," Salewa responds finally, and it is the truth. She is tired of it all. The pang in her stomach is a reminder that she drank the concentrated drink without food. What will be dinner? What will be breakfast? What is tomorrow? Is the girl real? Is Nengi real? Salewa wants to close her eyes, rest her head on the street that has betrayed her. She shakes the fog away and stares at her orange. She extends it to Nengi. She hopes their hands touch. "You want?"

Nengi shakes her head. "No, thank you. I haven't eaten, maybe I'll buy fried yam from those women."

Salewa's head swings in the direction Nengi is pointing. And there it is. While she watched the sun, the dusk market has come alive, in full swing. She sees the lanterns, flames licking their glass cages brown. She sees the goods: overflowing baskets of tatase peppers and onions, bright orange carrots and deep green okras, large plastic bowls of melon seeds and rusty tins of crayfish. All the colors are hyperreal. She sees the women, their indigo adire wrappers, the bold patterns of their ankara boubous, their chatter, and someone is calling out her name, "Salewa! Salewa!" As if her attention is needed, like she is real, like she belongs.

MASQUERADE SEASON

PAULY SHOULD STICK TO THE MAJOR ROADS WHEN
walking home from his cousins' house. That's what his mother
warns, abstractly, routinely, every morning of this summer holiday when she drops him off. He always nods yes, but in this
one thing, he is a disobedient son. He's tried to take the major
roads home, but they are so noisy with the grumbling trucks and
the plaintive honks from all the cars competing to get ahead.
Pauly knows more scenic routes home, less noisy paths that wind
between large houses they'll never be able to afford and parks his
mother has no time to take him to. And when Pauly doesn't want
to take this leisurely walk home, there is a shortcut. If he dips
behind the mosque down the street from his cousins' house, scurries across the gutter bridge made of two wooden planks, slashes
through some distance of overgrown bush, then hops over the
abandoned rusty back gate of Alele Estate, he will burst out two
streets away from home. The security guards at Alele's main gate
never question his passage; they wave at his sweaty forehead and
smile at the grass stains he's accumulated on the shorts his mother
makes for him.

Pauly is trying to get home quickly today. He stayed too long,

playing ball with his cousins, Ekene and John, in their huge backyard bordered by coconut trees. Behind the mosque, he star-
tles a man at his prayers. The man stills, following Pauly's path
through the backyard as his head hovers inches above the mat.
Pauly whispers an apology, not slowing down. He doesn't doubt
that the rotting planks will hold his weight, and across the makeshift bridge he goes. But today, a few steps into the bush, he stalls,
almost tripping, because here are three masquerades swaying in
front of him, blocking his path. Pauly is not aware of any masquerade festivals at this time of the year; he takes a small step
back, contemplating the out-of-context figures.

"Excuse me, please," he says, because his mother has taught
him to be polite.

The masquerades don't respond. They stand there, moving
left to right, then left, like backup singers at church. Pauly has to
tilt his head all the way behind to see the tops of their heads. The
first masquerade is the tallest, even taller than his science teacher,
who is a very tall six foot four—a detail the man crows at his short
students. The tall masquerade has a body of long raffia threads
layered over each other—as if someone has stacked fifty-six
brooms and topped them all with a brown cowboy hat, the kind
Woody in *Toy Story* wears. It has no face. The second masquerade is just a little taller than Pauly's mother. It is draped in rich
aso-oke, the bloodiest of reds. Pauly gawks at the twinkling beads
sewn into the cloth, dangling and scattering light, but his attention cannot stay long away from its square silver face with twin
black elliptical slits above three gashes of tribal marks on each
cheek. Though the head of the third masquerade is a solid dark
wood that takes up half its body length (with a chiseled triangle
nose, engraved circles for eyes, carved zigzags for teeth), there is

an explosion of colorful feathers around it. The feathers are blue and purple and red and yellow and pink and they are long and different, as if all the birds of the world have donated feathers for this purpose. Its skirt is made of several panels of cloth, each with an elaborate embroidered pattern.

When they keep shifting with the wind, not responding, Pauly moves to go around them. They don't stop him. How strange, he thinks, and keeps running; but isn't that a rustling following him? Pauly swings around and the masquerades halt, only a few steps behind.

"Why are you following me?" Pauly asks.

It is the feathered masquerade that speaks; the voice is a whispery, susurrating sound, as if the feathers themselves are speaking. The masquerade says, "Because we are your masquerades."

In the middle of this bush path, a shortcut to Pauly's home, he thinks how he has never owned anything so special and vivid and big. His mother will be proud. His cousins will be impressed.

"Okay," Pauly says, and takes them home, checking over his shoulder at every corner to make sure they are still there, tall and conspicuous and all his.

◊ ◊ ◊

THE MASQUERADES ARE SWOOSHING in the corner of the living room, between the old TV with the crooked antennae and the heat-trapping velvet curtains Pauly's mother keeps forgetting to replace. The masquerades are so bright, too bright maybe, for the otherwise dim apartment, and Pauly, seated on the edge of the sofa, sometimes has to look away, afraid his eyes will rupture from color.

It wasn't hard getting the masquerades home. They moved through the bush without incident, hopped over the gate gracefully—as if they were featherlight; when the Alele security guards had seen Pauly and the masquerades approaching, they waved and asked: "And what do we have here?" To which Pauly replied, "These are my masquerades," and the masquerades had swayed and Pauly liked the way the guards nodded, touched their cap visors to show they were impressed.

His mother has warned him not to bring strangers home, yes. So, in this second thing, he is a disobedient son. But Pauly is sure she will understand that masquerades aren't things you pass up, especially when they belong to you. And isn't it his mother who always says never to leave his belongings lying around? Never to lose them?

Pauly doesn't know what appropriate conversation with masquerades sounds like. Should he ask where they have come from? Would that be impolite? Would that be looking a gift horse in the mouth? Or should he ask what they do for fun? They don't look like they'd want to play football, staining their materials, which have somehow stayed clean through that bush passage. But maybe he shouldn't presume. Are they similar to pets he has to feed?

He finally speaks up. "Can I offer you biscuit and water?"

The red aso-oke masquerade bends forward, cloth rippling like a wave, then straightens. This voice is soft too, but more slippery, silkier than the feathered masquerade's. "Palm oil," the masquerade says from behind its silver mask.

"You want palm oil?"

"Yes," it says, the *s* slinking out, drawing long. "Only palm oil."

Pauly's mother arrives from her seamstress job in the middle of this conversation.

"Oh," she says when she steps into the room, lugging bags of vegetables and fish for dinner in one hand and bolts of fabric in the other. She stands there for a long moment, looking at the masquerades, her body not quite in or out. "Oh," she repeats. "We have company?"

"These are my masquerades," Pauly announces. He stands tall, all of his ten-year-old height. He spreads his hands toward them, as if they are an art project of his making. He waits for his mother to be impressed.

But she says nothing, just enters the living room fully, shutting the door with her foot. She walks past them to the kitchen and dumps her purchases on the counter. She is in there for a few minutes while Pauly squints at his masquerades, wondering if their sparkle has somehow muted, wondering how she is not standing beside him, in awe of these shades and textures.

She reappears at the door to the kitchen, holding a knife. "Does this mean I have to make dinner for five?"

"No," Pauly answers, happy not to add to her troubles. "They only eat palm oil."

"Good," his mother says, returning into the relative darkness of the kitchen. "Good," Pauly's mother repeats. "Because I'm tired."

◊ ◊ ◊

PAULY'S COUSINS WANT TO KNOW what the masquerades can do. They stand really close to the softly moving figures in their backyard, football suspended. The boys reach fingers out to touch Pauly's masquerades, but withdraw within inches of actual contact.

"I don't think they need to do anything!" Pauly responds, annoyed that the boys cannot just glory in the glistening of the beads, the luster of the raffia, the vibrancy of the feathers. "They're masquerades."

That first night had been weird, having the masquerades in his room, stuck in the corner with all his action figures and Legos. But after he had startled awake several times, the rustling of the first masquerade's raffia began to soothe him; the moon snuck in through a gap in his curtains and passed through the beads on the aso-oke, and they refracted light, dotting the walls and ceiling of Pauly's room with stars; the embroidered patterns on the third masquerade's skirt seemed to him like complete stories in a secret language known only to him, the silver threads glinting alive in the night.

"Jeez, calm down," Ekene says now, walking away from Pauly and his masquerades. "They're cool and all, but if they're just going to stand there—"

"Whatever," Pauly says. He doesn't need to be here with his cousins when he has three masquerades. "I'm going home," he announces. The masquerades glide behind him, as if backing his decision.

On the streets, Pauly kicks pebbles. The masquerades are quiet and now he regrets leaving his cousins.

"But is there anything you *can* do?" he turns to ask.

At first, he is sure they are ignoring him, but then the red aso-oke masquerade does the wavy thing again, silver head bowing down, then lifting up. The raffia masquerade hops and spins around on the spot. The feathers on the third masquerade rise, like a bird getting ready for flight—the feathers stick out in their million directions and Pauly steps back.

The masquerades dance. Out in the street, they twirl and contort and somersault. Pauly feels transformed, transported to another world, a brighter one than his summer holiday has given him so far, more radiant than the heady rush of scoring a goal against Ekene. The masquerades feint left, then jerk right, they jump and fold and twist and spasm and feathers flutter and cloths flap and billow and beads clink and jangle and the plumes blur and raffia palms create a *ssshhh-shhshshshh* wind that is the background pulse of their dance.

PAULY'S MOTHER LEAVES HER sewing machine for the evening and comes to sit with him. He is watching a movie about a group of teenagers solving crimes with their pet dragon. Static horizontal lines flicker across the screen intermittently, eclipsing their adventures.

Pauly moves to sit on the floor beside his mother's legs, leans his head against them. It is rare that she pauses work to be with him. In this moment, he is happy. The masquerades are next to the TV, swaying as usual. There is an almost-empty bowl of palm oil at their feet. It is Pauly's favorite bowl, the one with the robots holding hands. Pauly had spent a huge chunk of his afternoon staring at the bowl of palm oil, trying to catch them eating, but whenever he looked away or dozed off, he found the oil depleted. Now, he allows them their privacy and mystery.

He has his masquerades; he has his mother: it is a tranquillity Pauly revels in.

His mother runs her hand over his head slowly. "Pauly?"

"Mhmm?" The idyllic moment is lulling him to sleep.

"I'm working on this project now. I'm making a dress for that Nini Edoh actress. You've heard of her? It's for an awards show."

Pauly shrugs.

"Well, she's a big deal. And if she likes this dress, I will get plenty of clients and maybe we can move to a bigger house, you know, with a big backyard where you and Ekene and John can play football."

"That sounds nice," Pauly drawls, his voice slurring.

"But I need something from you."

"From me?" Pauly perks up. His mother expects things from him—to be polite, to wash the dishes, to be home before she returns from work—but she has never *needed* anything from him. He wipes sleep away. "What?"

"I think the raffia on your masquerade would make a wonderful belt. I need just a little bit of it, you know. I've never seen raffia like that before. It's so shiny and smooth! It will really pop against the orange of the dress." His mother sounds out of breath; it makes Pauly wince.

He turns to look at his mother; the TV lights are traveling over her face and he can see her stare fixed on the masquerades' corner, and Pauly understands it is them she's been watching all along. "Oh, I don't know," he says. "You'll have to ask them."

"But they're your masquerades," Pauly's mother reminds him. "You can do whatever you want."

Pauly crawls to kneel in front of the masquerade his mother is eyeing. The raffia really is lush and long and lustrous; Pauly has always known this. "Can I talk to them first?" he asks his mother.

"Of course, of course," his mother says, leaving the room.

Pauly cannot look up at the raffia masquerade's visage. He stares instead at its bottom, where its feet would be, the raffia threads sweeping against the floor in slow motion. "Is it okay if my mum takes some of your threads?" he asks. "I'll make sure it's not too much. She needs it for her job."

The raffia masquerade keeps moving, never still; it says, "We are your masquerades." Its voice is like a drum, deep and reverberating through Pauly's chest.

"Okay," Pauly says, and calls his mother in.

She is already holding a pair of scissors, and she is smiling as she approaches them. She is gentle with the masquerade, smoothing a hand over it the way she had rubbed Pauly's head, weighing the threads, sifting through them, smiling wider. "Yes, this will do very well," she says, and when her scissors snip loudly, Pauly looks away.

◊ ◊ ◊

PAULY ISN'T SURE IF he is seeing this right, but the next day, it looks like the raffia masquerade is leaning a little, tilting, no longer as tall as his science teacher. Are the feathers of the third masquerade wilting? Is the aso-oke of the second masquerade duller, less red? When he pours from the keg of palm oil into their bowl, he keeps pouring until it overflows, the red oil running across the bowl's illustrated robot hands.

Pauly's mother comes home around noon, earlier than ever. She says the actress loved the belt and has referred her services to all her friends. Pauly's mother is so happy, grinning so wide that her pink gums are exposed. She wants to take him to Sweet Sensation to celebrate. Pauly is excited. They haven't been out to eat in forever. He wears his favorite sneakers, he brushes his tight coils; then he and the masquerades stand by the door, waiting.

"Oh, Pauly," his mother says when she emerges from her room, applying lipstick, dangling her car keys, "I don't think your masquerades should come. This is mother-son time, and the restaurant might be crowded."

Pauly looks to the masquerades, and before he asks, there is that soft voice saying, "We are your masquerades." And Pauly knows he can tell them to stay. He does. "Stay," he says, and his mother takes his hand.

At the restaurant, when Pauly's mother says yes to him getting both ice cream and an egg roll alongside his yamarita, everything tastes chalky. He swallows hard as his mother calls him her good and perfect and obedient son. He nods at his mother's promises: a new house, a new bicycle, more time together.

◇ ◇ ◇

PAULY GUIDES HIS MASQUERADES on a tour through one of the neighborhoods where he takes his leisurely strolls. They noiselessly follow him through the cleaner streets with the tall palm trees, and grass that looks too green to be real. The raffia masquerade is still tilting, but not by much. The colors seem to have replenished themselves in the feathers, in the aso-oke. Pauly is glad.

"Look," he says, pointing at the white house with two fat columns holding up a balcony. The wrought-iron gate surrounding the compound is painted gold. "We can have a house like that and we can all stand up there and look down at the street and there will be space to dance in the backyard and play football."

The masquerades sway beside him, silent.

◊ ◊ ◊

WHEN PAULY'S MOTHER ASKS for a strip of the red aso-oke, Pauly starts to cry.

"Why are you crying?" she asks, folding herself to sit next to him on the floor. She strokes his head; the smell of her stale sweat mixed with the smell of the lubricant she uses for her sewing machine envelops him.

"It's not fair!" Pauly says.

His mother leans back, away from him. "Not fair?"

"They don't like it," he explains. "They didn't like it when you cut before."

"Did they tell you that?" And when he doesn't respond to this, his mother goes on: "They are yours. You can do what you want. What will a little bit of fabric hurt?" She turns to look at the masquerade beside the TV. "Look at that thing." Her voice sounds breathy again. "It probably has up to forty yards of aso-oke on it. I'm asking for only half a yard, Pauly."

Pauly cries harder. He can still hear the snip of the first cut, can see the way the masquerade tilted afterward. "I don't . . . want you . . . to do it." Hiccups punctuate his sentence.

"See, it's a big woman who wants this dress that I'm making o. She is Iyaloja of Balogun. Do you know what that means?"

Pauly shakes his head.

"It means that if this goes well, we've made it. I get an in with their market association. Look, Pauly, don't you want me to spend more time at home? Don't you want Ekene and John to come over, instead of you always going there? This single mother life is so hard, Pauly, I just want us to be happy. I want things to be easier for us both."

Pauly cries some more as he nods, and his tears blur so that the scissors going through the red aso-oke look like a knife slicing through blood.

◊ ◊ ◊

ON THE WAY TO his cousins' house, Pauly begs his masquerades to dance.

The masquerades bend and rise, as if bowing again to Pauly, but they do not jump and twirl and somersault this time. They sway, at first slowly, and then faster. They sway left and right, their heads almost touching the ground before they go in the reverse direction. The feathers do not spread out in glorious performance; they droop behind the wooden head. The cowboy hat has a crooked rim. The silver face doesn't reflect the sun; the slits darken. There is no crackling of raffia, no clinking of beads; there is silence as they move through this muted dance, this slouching, mournful dance that makes Pauly want to cry. "Stop," he whispers, and they do.

When he gets to his cousins' house, they are dressed to follow *him* home. Apparently, his mother has called ahead, mentioning a surprise.

They all walk back to Pauly's house, using the major roads. Pedestrians stop to stare and frown at these wilting masquerades. Pauly wishes his hands were wide enough, that he were big enough to protect them from these looks, to gather them into his arms and console them.

In Pauly's living room is a new TV. It is flat and slick and takes up most of the wall. The masquerades glide to their corner, which is now half of what it used to be. Pauly flinches at how cramped they look, feathers sticking into aso-oke and aso-oke cloaking raffia and raffia tangling with feathers. But the TV comes on, and for the first time, the hues on the TV are brighter than Pauly's three masquerades.

◊ ◊ ◊

PAULY'S MOTHER KNOCKS ON his room door and he knows what she wants.

"It's the governor's wife, Pauly!" She sounds excited, her voice pitching higher as it reaches Pauly through the wood.

He doesn't respond. The masquerades are by his toys. They are still swaying, but barely, like they are tired.

"I just need a few feathers, my darling boy. I'm doing a neck detail that will stun everybody! This is it, Pauly! I can feel it. Our lives are about to change!"

Pauly climbs down from his bed, softly, so his mother doesn't hear his movements. He slowly pushes Legos aside so that there is space to sit in front of them. He buries his head in his palms and they all bend, his masquerades, they swoop low and around him. He can feel all their textures tickling his neck, brushing his arms, rubbing his head.

"Are you sleeping, Pauly? I know you're not sleeping. Open this door! You're being disobedient! You're ignoring your mother!"

Pauly stays quiet in the cocoon of his masquerades.

"I just want what's best for us, Pauly." She knocks again. "Okay, I'll make you pancakes for breakfast in the morning and we can talk about it."

His mother shuffles away and Pauly remains in their embrace. He knows now that it will never end. A feather here, two yards of aso-oke there, three more raffia threads—until there will be nothing of them left.

◊ ◊ ◊

PAULY LIES AWAKE THAT NIGHT, watching the beads of the aso-oke refract stars across his face. He listens to the *ssshhh-shhshhh* of the rustling raffia masquerade. He traces the stories on the feather masquerade's skirt. Pauly doesn't sleep.

◊ ◊ ◊

AT FIRST MORNING LIGHT, Pauly and his masquerades slip out of the house. It is a somber walk to the bush where Pauly first encountered them. The security guards of Alele Estate are asleep on duty. They walk past their snores.

Pauly stands opposite his masquerades in the bush. A bulb behind the mosque shines light through the dim dawn, glinting off the beads, falling on the woven texture of the aso-oke, highlighting the colors of the feathers.

"You have to go," Pauly says to his masquerades. He has to stay with his mother, be her obedient son, but why should they have to sacrifice themselves for an ideal lifestyle?

The masquerades do not go. They sway in front of him.

"We are your masquerades," they say together, breathy and silky and reverberating.

Behind Pauly, the muezzin's call to prayer rings out, a long-held note rising and dipping.

"Then you have to obey," Pauly says. "You have to go."

Still, they don't leave. They shuffle closer to Pauly, sinuous, silent.

"You have to go!"

"We are your masquerades." Their movement intensifies, becomes faster. They dip left, then right. "We are your masquerades."

"Please, go." Pauly's voice breaks into a whisper.

The fluid, drooping dance slows down and they bow, the tops of their heads brushing Pauly's; they crowd in, textures and patterns and colors surrounding the boy.

The rustling starts when they move away from him. Pauly doesn't want to watch, but he forces himself to. At first, they just keep swaying, slower, but then the raffia masquerade twirls and the feathers on the third masquerade rise, pointing in all the directions, and there—the beads are clinking again. The masquerades somersault and spin and contort, tones blurring, threads swishing, free and full, dancing into the morning sun.

ACKNOWLEDGMENTS

MY MOTHER TEASES THAT WHEN I WAS A BABY, I WAS
quite chunky, and that's why visitors hesitated to lift and hold me.
"You learned to play by yourself, content." She says I got so good
at this lonesome living, and maybe that's why the phone hardly
rang for me when I was a teenager, why I had few friends. These
days, she goes, "Where did all these people come from? How did
we get here?" I don't know, Mummy. But I'm hella grateful.

To my beloveds who believed earlier and harder than I
ever did. Subomi Laditan, my plus-one, who paid for my MFA
applications to prove it, for never doubting. Desola Falomo, for
showing me how to love, for grounding me. Tolu Talabi, for the
never-ending banter, and asking me the hard questions. IfeOluwa
Nihinlola, for the mini essays and snacks and gossip sessions.
Aderonke Taiwo, for taking care of me, even from miles away.

This world of writing has brought me into communion with
many wondrous talented humans. You've taught me to write bet-

ter, and these stories were improved from your input, one way or other. But beyond this, being your friend has taught me to be a fuller person; our conversations leave me enlightened and buoyant: Morgan Thomas, Gerardo Sámano Córdova, Charlie Sorrenson, Uche Okonkwo, Elinam Agbo, Meagean Dugger, Cherline Bazile, Daphne Andreades Palasi, Rafeeat Aliyu, Rochelle Marrett, Mariya Zilberman, Erika Nestor, Nishanth Injam, Rachel Girty, Akil Kumarasamy, Josha Nathan, Yohanca Delgado, Em North, Molly Bronstein, Laurie Thomas. How did I get so lucky? You inspire me. I love you all to bursting.

Ifeyinwa Arinze and Clarisse Baleja Saidi, thank you for our special sisterhood, for the guiding light of your brilliance. My dear friends Seun O., Douye F., Bolaji O., Simisola O., Tomisin O., Audrey E., Kovie P., Jolaade O., Peter C., the YM crew, my Miami boos, my Philly loves—look, we did it!

I'm so thankful to all the people who shared those three charmed years with me in Ann Arbor: the artists and scientists and the beef patty spot. The Helen Zell Writers' Program at the University of Michigan sounded like a dream when it came— three years of funded writing? Stuff of my wildest imaginations. I'm beholden to the faculty and staff, and especially to my cohort—Eirill, Elinam, Colin, Gerardo, Rachel G., Rachel C., David G., David W., Mant, Thea, Coleen—who read the messiest drafts of these stories, and shared so much vulnerability and laughter and talent in those long, narrow rooms.

To all my teachers and mentors and recommenders, in every context, who showed me what could be, and guided me here. To name a few: Mr. Oparaji of Dansol High School, who let me write stories for the essay prompts. Eileen Pollack and Peter Ho Davies, who assured me that I had something to say. Edwidge Danticat, for so much warmth and wisdom. Lesley Nneka Arimah, Jeff Vandermeer, Laura van den Berg, Michael Ray and Peter, for the advice, time, and testimonials.

I found true community at Clarion UCSD, Bread Loaf Writers' Conference, Aspen Summer Words, Juniper Summer Workshop, Farafina Workshop, and Tin House Summer Conference. In your presences, I felt the joy of creation, of belonging.

I have been lucky to be supported by a number of wonderful residencies and organizations: the Miami Book Fair, Deborah Rogers Foundation, MacDowell, Art Omi, Kimmel Harding Nelson Center for the Arts, Writivism, Lighthouse Works, Black Rock Senegal, I-Park Foundation, and James Merrill House. Thank you for the wildly talented people I broke bread with—and yes, the delicious meals—but I'm grateful for the quiet, particularly, for the gifts of woods and lakes and beaches and pools and space to listen to myself.

Thanks to the magazines and editors who took chances on these stories long before now: *Omenana, Granta, One Story, Zoetrope, Zyzzyva, Ploughshares, American Short Fiction, Nightmare,* and Tor.com; and to the anthologies and prizes that have recognized my stories over the years.

And to my readers, since Betty days and after, thanks for bugging me to write a book. And for the emails and tweets of encouragement while you waited impatiently.

Thank you to the writers who wrote books, so that I could write books.

Renée Zuckerbrot, my stalwart agent, I think you're cool. Thanks for your generosity, for moving mountains, for the pep talks, and for keeping the bar so very high. Thanks to Maria Massie, and everyone at MMQ Lit for consistently having my back. I am very grateful to Caspian Dennis and everyone at Abner Stein for holding down the fort in the UK. And to my film agents, Alice Lawson and Hannah Vaughn, for standing in my corner.

My editors and publishers—Nneoma Amadi-Obi and the Norton family, Anna Kelly and the Virago family, Othuke Ominiabohs and the Masobe family—thank you for choosing me.

I might not be here if my family didn't allow me to hog the bathroom for hours to read books in quiet. Fola, Modupe, Funmbi and Amiola—thank you for the prayers, for entertaining my strangeness, and the pride in your eyes. You're my why. My nieces, Imisi, Fiyin, Titobi, I want you to see that sometimes a girl dreams, and those dreams come true.

Yoruba people say, "Eniyan l'aṣọ," and how real that's been for me! I could keep writing pages, naming names. It is you all who have clothed me, covered me, cheered me on, and carried me here. Thank you.